John D.
Ruddy

John D. Ruddy, from Letterkenny, Co. Donegal, is a writer, actor, teacher, illustrator and historian. He is the creator of Manny Man and the YouTube history series Manny Man Does History, including World War I in 6 Minutes and Irish History in 6 Minutes. When not writing and illustrating history videos, John is usually treading the boards of the Irish stage as a professional actor or in the classroom teaching history.

Stay up to date with the author at:

 www.twitter.com/JohnDRuddy

 www.facebook.com/JohnDRuddy

 www.youtube.com/c/JohnDRuddyMannyMan

 www.instagram.com/johndruddy

Dedicated to my dad, Daniel, supporting
me in all my endeavours, passing on
his fascination with everything to me,
and putting the D. in John D. Ruddy!
Thanks, Dad!

MANNY MAN DOES REVOLUTIONARY IRELAND 1916-1923 BY JOHN D. RUDDY

The Collins Press

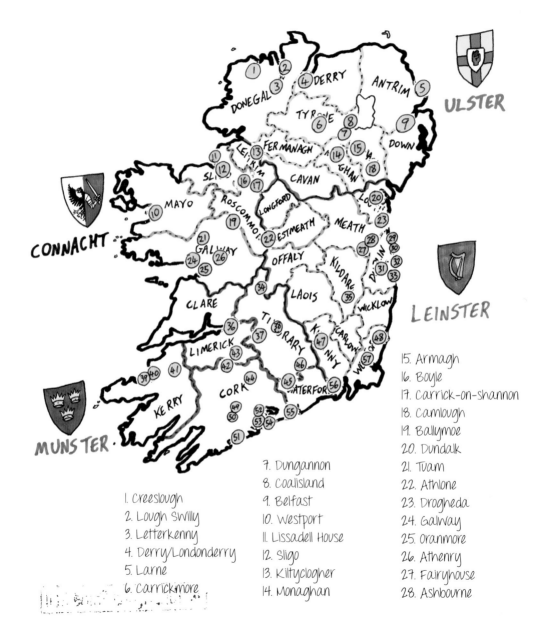

ULSTER

DONEGAL
1
2
3
4 DERRY
5
ANTRIM

TYRONE
6
7
8
9

FERMANAGH
13
14
15
18 DOWN
CAVAN

MONAGHAN

ULSTER

CONNACHT

MAYO
10

SLIGO
11
12
16
17

ROSCOMMON
19

LEITRIM

LONGFORD

20

MEATH
23
28
29
30
27

GALWAY
21
24
26
25

ATHLONE
22

WESTMEATH

OFFALY

DUBLIN
31
32
33

CONNACHT

CLARE

TIPPERARY
36
37
38

LIMERICK
43
42

KILDARE
35

LAOIS

KILKENNY
47
46

CARLOW

WICKLOW
48
57

WEXFORD

LEINSTER

34

39 40 41

KERRY

CORK
44
49
50
52
53 54 55
51

WATERFORD
45
56

MUNSTER

1. Creeslough
2. Lough Swilly
3. Letterkenny
4. Derry/Londonderry
5. Larne
6. Carrickmore

7. Dungannon
8. Coalisland
9. Belfast
10. Westport
11. Lissadell House
12. Sligo
13. Kiltyclogher
14. Monaghan

15. Armagh
16. Boyle
17. Carrick-on-Shannon
18. Camlough
19. Ballymoe
20. Dundalk
21. Tuam
22. Athlone
23. Drogheda
24. Galway
25. Oranmore
26. Athenry
27. Fairyhouse
28. Ashbourne

Foreword

In 2016 we commemorated the centenary of the Easter Rising, Ireland's strike for freedom. We all marked it in very different ways; we had parades, social events, art competitions, flag ceremonies and plays; personally, I read the Proclamation of Independence in front of Letterkenny Post Office to a small and slightly confused crowd on Easter Monday. But as much as 2014 marked the centenary of only the beginning of the First World War, so too did 2016 mark the centenary of only the beginning of big change in Ireland. It was the first domino to fall in an ever-accelerating push for Irish freedom. As the years go on, we hit the centenaries of the Irish War of Independence and the Civil War, the latter a much more bitter and complicated conflict which won't be as simple to commemorate. While all of these commemorations go on, it is important to have a good knowledge of what it was all about before it is lost in a sea of analysis, hindsight and political posturing. I give you Manny Man Does Revolutionary Ireland: 1916–1923!

Leabharlanna Fhine Gall

15000 BCE–1066 CE Isles of Invasions

Out on the western edge of Europe, the little island of Ireland had waves of invasions. The Celts became dominant in Ireland around 2,500 years ago. Then Vikings came from Scandinavia around 1,200 years ago. Some were violent, some stayed and integrated into the Irish life and brought some of their own skills, traditions and culture.

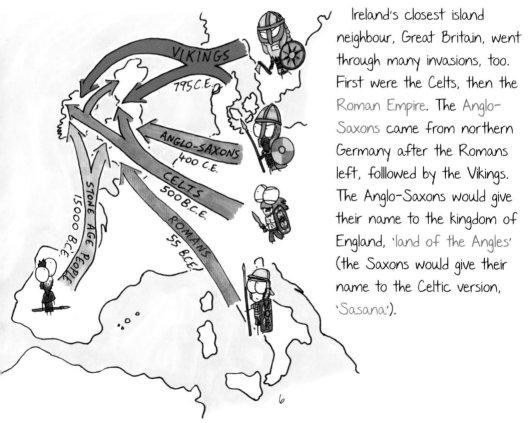

Ireland's closest island neighbour, Great Britain, went through many invasions, too. First were the Celts, then the Roman Empire. The Anglo-Saxons came from northern Germany after the Romans left, folllowed by the Vikings. The Anglo-Saxons would give their name to the kingdom of England, 'land of the Angles' (the Saxons would give their name to the Celtic version, 'Sasana').

Richard de Clare aka Strongbow

The Ulster Plantation

PRIVATELY PLANTED ALREADY

In 1066, new invaders came to England: the Normans, ironclad warriors on horseback from Normandy in northern France. They conquered England swiftly and established a strong kingdom of stone castles and fortresses. In 1170 they came to Ireland to help an Irish king in his wars. The Norman Richard de Clare, aka 'Strongbow', became king of Leinster and thus began English rule in Ireland. Successive English monarchs made laws and waged wars to divide the people living in Ireland, Gaelic and Norman.

England began to establish colonies across the world in the 17th century, and also established plantations in Ulster. There was now a religious divide between the Irish and English, Catholic and Protestant. In the 1650s, Catholics were kicked off their land, ensuring a minority Protestant ruling class in Ireland. The Penal Laws were brought in to clamp down on Catholic rights and also the rights of Presbyterians, another Protestant Church. They were all to conform to the Anglican Church, the Church of England.

To Hell or to Connacht

7

Nine Years' War

1770s–1800s The Birth of Irish Republicanism

The end of the 18th century saw the American and French Revolutions and the birth of their Republics. Instead of being ruled by a monarch, they would be run by a government democratically elected by the people. This idea of Republicanism in Ireland grew amongst the Society of United Irishmen. Groups like the Orange Order were set up to oppose this move for independence.

Emblem of the United Irishmen

Theobald Wolfe Tone of the United Irishmen and the father of Irish Republicanism thought a rebellion was needed to establish an Irish Republic.

The rebellion in 1798, however, was defeated and Wolfe Tone died, but the dream of an Irish Republic did not die with him.

Members of the early Orange Order

Theobald Wolfe Tone

After the rebellion, Ireland was ruled directly from London and became part of the United Kingdom in the Acts of Union of 1801. In 1803, Robert Emmet led a quickly quelled republican rebellion in Dublin and was later executed. British rule would not be questioned! Ireland was but another part of the ever-growing British Empire.

1801

UNITED KINGDOM OF GREAT BRITAIN AND IRELAND

The Acts of Union created the United Kingdom

1840s–1860s

When the Potato Famine hit Ireland in
the 1840s, millions died or left, many

potato blight

never to return. The parliament in London did little to
help. Before the Famine the population of Ireland was
around 8 million but by the 1890s it was only 1 million.
There were more Irish living in America than there were
in Ireland. Anger festered and rumblings of an Irish
Republic grew again.

The many
people
leaving
Ireland

Young Ireland was an early Irish Nationalist group in
the 1840s. It was they who unveiled the Irish tricolour
for the first time, Green for the Republicans, White for
Peace and Orange for the Unionist North. After a small
failed rebellion in 1848, the Young Irelanders ultimately
dissolved. Former member John O'Mahony later founded
the Fenian Brotherhood in America while James
Stephens founded the Irish Republican Brotherhood
(IRB) in Dublin. These two secret organisations worked
together to establish an Irish Republic.

John O'Mahony

ERIN GO BRAGH!

James Stephens and the IRB

The Irish tricolour

Many Irish arrived in America
to start a new life

Passing the Republic on

Jeremiah O'Donovan Rossa

The Fenians believed the Republic must be achieved through force. Cork-born Fenian leader Jeremiah O'Donovan Rossa and others were imprisoned for planning a Fenian rebellion in 1865. The rebellion later in 1867 was poorly organised and ultimately didn't amount to much; the British had been tipped off by informants, a weakness often exploited by the British.

After his release, Jeremiah O'Donovan Rossa travelled to America, an exile. He linked up with the Fenians there and began to plot. He decided that dynamite, a new invention, could be used to great effect to wake up the British government to the Irish plight. Young Fenians were trained to use the dynamite and would then cross the Atlantic to carry out a bombing campaign across the UK. One of these young Fenians was future Easter Rising leader Thomas Clarke.

Flag flown during the ill-fated 1867 Rebellion

GOD SAVE IRELAND
ANGLESBORO '67

10

The Gaelic Revival

The late 19th century also saw a revival of Gaelic traditions that had been waning. Conradh na Gaeilge (Gaelic League) was set up in 1893 by Douglas Hyde and Eoin MacNeill to promote the Irish language, which was literally being beaten out of children in the classroom. This organisation attracted many Irish Nationalists, proud of their own country, and it was the perfect recruitment ground for the IRB. Teacher and poet Patrick Pearse and uileann piper Éamonn Ceannt were members. Conradh na Gaeilge published a newspaper called 'An Claidheamh Soluis' ('The Sword of Light') with Pearse as editor from 1903 to 1909.

Logo of An Claidheamh Soluis

Eoin MacNeill and Douglas Hyde

Home Rule v. The Ulster Covenant

WE WANT HOME RULE!!!

Charles Stewart Parnell

Arthur Griffith

The rise in Irish Nationalism led to demand for Home Rule, for parliament to be in Dublin once more. Isaac Butt set up the Home Rule League in 1873 which became the Irish Parliamentary Party (IPP) under Charles Stewart Parnell in the 1880s. Where the IRB wanted to achieve Irish independence through force, the IPP wanted to achieve it through parliament in London. Dublin writer Arthur Griffith thought Irish members of parliament should not go to London and he set up the Sinn Féin ('We Ourselves') party in 1905. The Protestant Unionists, centred mainly in Ulster, considered themselves British, not Irish, and were quite happy with the Union of Great Britain and Ireland. Most of the major industry was in Ulster and they believed a Dublin parliament would be ruled by the Catholic Church. In 1912, thousands of Unionists across Ulster, led by Edward Carson and James Craig, vowed to fight against Home Rule by signing the Ulster Covenant.

Sinn Féin looking to hold Ireland together

Westminster Palace – Home of the British Parliament in London

The Signing of the Ulster Covenant

James Connolly

WHY DO WE HAVE TO SHOOT POOR IRISH PEOPLE?

Young Connolly in the British Army

The Plough and the Stars – The flag of socialism in Ireland

James Connolly

James Connolly was born in Edinburgh, Scotland, in 1868 to Irish parents. He grew up in the slums, surrounded by other poor working-class Irish families living in Edinburgh. He left school at 10 and when he was 14, he lied his way into the British Army. He was stationed in Ireland where he met Lillie Reynolds, the woman he would one day marry. At that time (the 1880s), there was unrest in rural Ireland as poor Irish farmers were organising against their landlords in what was known as the Land League. The British Army was often deployed to bring law and order and Connolly grew to hate it. When his regiment was to be transferred to India, Connolly deserted and moved with Lillie back to Scotland where they started a family. There he got involved in the socialist movement, standing up for the working class. His work in socialism brought him and his family to Dublin where he shaped the Irish Socialist Republican Party.

1913 The Dublin Lockout

Liberty Hall

In the 1900s, Dublin had some of the poorest living conditions in Europe. Many families lived in cramped conditions in tenement buildings. Dock workers were at the mercy of their employers. Any talk of coming together or unionising could get you blacklisted and not be able to get any more work! Socialist James Larkin helped them form a union and, with James Connolly, he set up the Labour Party as Home Rule began to approach. Larkin and Connolly would lead the workers on strike to demand better pay and working conditions.

In August 1913, 300 employers locked out 20,000 Dublin workers and brought in workers from elsewhere, leaving the poor people of Dublin with no income to feed their families. During protests, the Dublin Metropolitan Police weren't too gentle with the protesters so Connolly set up the Irish Citizen Army to protect them. The lockout ended in January 1914 in defeat: the poor people went back to work, promising not to unionise.

THE GREAT APPEAR GREAT BECAUSE WE ARE ON OUR KNEES! LET US RISE!!

MURPHY MUST GO!

DON'T WEAR CLOTHES MADE BY SCAB LABOUR!

James Larkin during the Dublin Lockout

Thomas Clarke

Thomas Clarke

Tom Clarke was born in the south of England in 1858 but grew up in Dungannon, Co. Tyrone. He joined the IRB at the age of 20 and, after an attack on the police, he fled to America. There he became involved in Jeremiah O'Donovan Rossa's dynamite plan for England. Clarke was sent to London in 1883 to blow up London Bridge but was arrested and jailed for 15 years. In 1898 he moved to New York where he married Kathleen Daly. They moved to Dublin in 1907 where Clarke opened a tobacco shop at the top of Sackville (now O'Connell) Street and held secret IRB meetings in the back. Being an IRB veteran by now, he began working with the younger members, such as Bulmer Hobson and Séan Mac Diarmada. The IRB was growing in Ireland and Clarke would be there to guide the way.

WHAT CAN I HELP YOU WITH? TOBACCO? A NEWSPAPER? AN IRISH REPUBLIC?

ᚈ. S. Ó'CLÉIRIS

SMOKE GALLAHER'S TWO FLAKES TOBACCO AND GOLD PLATE CIGARETTES

75ᴬ

BRANCH OF ANGERS ST

TOBACCO STATIONARY

NOTE: **SMOKING KILLS!!**

Clarke's tobacco shop across from the Parnell Monument

Bulmer Hobson and Séan Mac Diarmada

1913 Rise of the Volunteers

HOME RULE WILL BE WAITING FOR YOU WHEN YOU GET HOME!

John Redmond

In 1913, while John Redmond of the IPP was continuing to push Home Rule in the British Parliament, the Unionists in the North who had signed the Covenant set up the Ulster Volunteers to defend their loyalty to Britain. They smuggled rifles from Germany into Larne, Co. Antrim, and began arming themselves. In reaction, Irish Nationalists in the South formed the Irish Volunteers. They too ran guns, into Howth just north of Dublin. Tensions were running high and Ireland was on the brink of civil war. If Home Rule was passed, the Ulster Volunteers would go to war. Having been a convicted criminal, Thomas Clarke stayed out of direct involvement with the Irish Volunteers but seeing other IRB members such as Hobson and Mac Diarmada join up, he was reassured the Volunteers were in good Republican hands.

ULSTER VOLUNTEERS

IRISH VOLUNTEERS

Patrick Pearse

Patrick Pearse was born in Dublin in 1879. He grew up around the corner from Trinity College and from a very young age became very proud of his Irish identity. As a young man, he worked with his brother, Willie, for their father, James, who

Patrick Pearse

CÚCHULAINN
2000 BCE (MYTHOLOGY)

THEOBALD WOLFE TONE
1798

ROBERT EMMET
1803

was a stonemason from England. Growing up right in the middle of the Gaelic Revival, Pearse became a great advocate for the Irish language, joining Conradh na Gaeilge. He took great inspiration from the ancient Celtic legendary warrior Cúchulainn, as well as past Republican leaders Theobald Wolfe Tone and Robert Emmet. Pearse was a barrister, a poet

ANOIS A BHUACHAILLÍ, ABAIR LIOM É: TABHAIR DÚINN ÁR DTÍR AR AIS ARÍS LE BHUR DTOIL!

St Enda's in Rathfarnham

and a teacher. He set up a bilingual school for boys, St Enda's, in Dublin. Pearse had a turn in his eye which is why he insisted on being photographed from the side. Not only was it an iconic pose, it was also a self-conscious one! When the Irish Volunteers formed in 1913, Pearse joined up and, shortly after, joined the IRB too. He quickly moved up the ranks as Tom Clarke saw great leadership potential in Pearse.

1914 The Great War in Europe

The trenches of France and Belgium

The split in the Irish Volunteers

NOW IS THE TIME TO STRIKE!!

WE'LL COME BACK STRONGER!

In London, John Redmond of the Irish Parliamentary Party saw the Home Rule Bill passed in May 1914, but later that summer, the Great War began. Home Rule was put on hold while the British fought Germany. Redmond told the Irish Volunteers that now was the time to go out and fight for Home Rule ... in the trenches of France and Belgium. He thought that Irish soldiers could train in the British Army and eventually return to be a fully fledged army for an Ireland ruled from home. The war was expected to last until Christmas. Little did he know of the horrors to be found in the trenches. A total of 170,000 Volunteers agreed with Redmond, but 11,000 did not. These Volunteers, such as Pearse and Mac Diarmada, thought this was a betrayal and believed that now was the time to strike. IRB members began planning an uprising. England's difficulty was Ireland's opportunity ... and the war in Europe went on for another five years!

UM YEA... HOME RULE WILL HAVE TO WAIT.

OK...

Redmond's interference and the split in the Volunteers led to secrets being held from fellow members. Bulmer Hobson's support of Redmond led to Hobson falling out with the IRB command. Patrick Pearse, Éamonn Ceannt, Thomas McDonagh and Joseph Plunkett had important positions within the Irish Volunteers but were also all IRB members, so the IRB was still secretly calling the shots from the inside. In May 1915 they set up a Military Council and were joined by Tom Clarke and Séan Mac Diarmada. Secrecy was key to the planning. Not even Eoin MacNeill, chief of staff of the Volunteers, was aware of the plotting.

The Secret Military Council began to meet

The split went deep

1915 Funeral of O'Donovan Rossa

Old Fenian leader Jeremiah O'Donovan Rossa died in America later that summer. The IRB used this as a great opportunity to rally support. They had his body sent home to Ireland and held a huge funeral in Glasnevin Cemetery in Dublin. Patrick Pearse, the new young face of Irish Republicanism, made a rousing graveside oration. Talking about the British, he said: 'The fools! The fools! The fools! They have left us our Fenian dead, and while Ireland still holds these graves, Ireland unfree shall never be at peace!' It was a not-so-subtle declaration of intent! Clarke, Pearse and the secret Military Council decided that their rebellion would be on Easter Sunday 1916, a symbolic day of resurrection and new life.

Jeremiah O'Donovan Rossa died in New York in June 1915

IRELAND UNFREE SHALL NEVER BE AT PEACE!!

Pearse delivering his rousing graveside oration

THAT'S OUR MAN!

Republican Leaders

Seán Mac Diarmada was born near Kiltyclogher, Co. Leitrim, in 1883. He moved to Dublin in his 20s and quickly got involved in Sinn Féin, Conradh na Gaeilge and the IRB. He helped set up a newspaper called 'Irish Freedom'. Through the IRB, he became a protégé of Tom Clarke. He travelled the country speaking out in public against the British, which got him into trouble with the authorities. Mac Diarmada suffered from polio so he walked with a cane.

Seán Mac Diarmada

The logo of the 'Irish Freedom' newspaper

Coat of arms of the National University of Ireland

Thomas McDonagh was born in Cloughjordan, Co. Tipperary, in 1878. An academic and poet, he was a professor of French, English and Latin. His love of the Irish language led him to teach in Pearse's St Enda's School. The two men were good friends. McDonagh was one of the founders of ASTI, the secondary school teacher trade union in Ireland. He married Muriel Gifford in 1912 and they had two children. He became involved with the Irish Volunteers and his Republicanism was deepened by the IRB.

Thomas McDonagh

Joseph Plunkett

Joseph Mary Plunkett was born in Fitzwilliam Street, Dublin, in 1887 to a very wealthy family. He suffered from tuberculosis so he spent a lot of his childhood in the warmer climates of the Mediterranean and North Africa. When he joined Conradh na Gaeilge, Thomas McDonagh became his tutor. They shared an interest in writing poetry and in the theatre. Plunkett became engaged to McDonagh's sister-in-law Grace Gifford. While on the secret Military Council, Plunkett began to forge a plan of action.

ALL YOU NEED IS A BIT OF ELBOW GREASE!

Éamonn Ceannt playing the uilleann pipes

Éamonn Ceannt was born in Ballymoe, Co. Galway, in 1881. When he was very young his family moved to Co. Louth and after his father retired as a policeman of the Royal Irish Constabulary (RIC) they moved to Dublin in 1892. Ceannt became heavily involved in Conradh na Gaeilge and began teaching the Irish language. He was also a very talented and successful player of the uilleann pipes and he set up the Pipers Club to help revive Irish traditional music. He met his wife, Áine Ní Bhaonáin, through Conradh na Gaeilge. They had one son.

22

LIBERTY HALL

WE SERVE NEITHER KING NOR KAISER BUT IRELAND

HEAD OFFICE IRISH TRANSPORT AND GENERAL WORKERS UNION

Connolly and the Irish Citizen Army

While all the secret plotting was going on, James Connolly had other plans. In protest against the imperialist war in Europe, he hung a banner outside his headquarters at Liberty Hall: 'We serve neither King nor Kaiser but Ireland!' Believing the Republicans were all bark and no bite, Connolly and his Citizen Army threatened to fight the British themselves at the start of 1916. The IRB quickly brought him into the fold before he did something rash and destroyed all their carefully laid plans. Connolly became part of the Military Council and the IRB gained another small army. Thomas McDonagh would be next to join the Military Council.

Connolly threatening an uprising of his own

WHAT ABOUT THE WORKING PEOPLE? SOMETHING REAL NEEDS DOING!!

TO WAR!!!

NO, WAIT!!! WE'VE GOT SOMETHING PLANNED FOR EASTER!!

Cumann na mBan

Cumann na mBan (or The Irishwomen's Council) were akin to the suffragette movement of the time, fighting for women's rights. Women at this time did not have the right to vote. Cumann na mBan was founded in Wynn's Hotel, Dublin, in 1914 to help assist the Irish Volunteers in the approach of Home Rule, by force of arms if necessary. When the Great War broke out in Europe, most of Cumann na mBan sided with the Irish Volunteers against Redmond. The women of Cumann na mBan were of a very diverse background coming from many walks of life.

CUMANN NA MBAN
(THE IRISHWOMEN'S COUNCIL)

Constance Markievicz

Constance Gore-Booth, daughter of an Arctic explorer, was born in 1868 and grew up in Lissadell House, Co. Sligo. She was friends with poet W. B. Yeats while living there. She married a wealthy Polish artist and became Countess Markievicz. She came to Dublin in 1903 and became involved in many political and cultural movements. She was involved in Inghinidhe na hÉireann ('Daughters of Ireland') a precursor of Cumann na mBan begun by Maud Gonne. Markievicz and Bulmer Hobson set up Fianna Éireann, a youth organisation involved with the Irish Volunteers and the IRB. She performed with Maud Gonne in the Abbey Theatre, the national theatre founded by her friend W. B. Yeats along with J. M. Synge and Lady Gregory. Markievicz was passionately involved with socialism and joined the Irish Citizen Army. She had great respect for James Connolly.

As the Rising approached, Cumann na mBan were also brought into the plan.

W. B. Yeats and the Abbey Theatre

1916 Planning The Rising

Volunteers out on manoeuvres

The plan was for the Irish Volunteers to go out on manoeuvres and parades on Easter Sunday 1916. Pearse had arranged this with the organisation. Publicly, this was acceptable to British authorities as well as to Volunteers such as Eoin MacNeill who were against any sort of uprising. Only the higher-up IRB members would know that the manoeuvres were to be the real deal. When the Volunteers went out on Easter Sunday, IRB leaders would direct their Volunteers to capture strategic spots across the country. The British would be taken by surprise while they were concentrating on the trenches of France and Belgium. The Volunteers would hold the island and declare an Irish Republic. Joseph Plunkett used his limited military knowledge to make out the plan. What could really boost their cause would be German reinforcements, and they had a man over there organising them!

England's difficulty would be Ireland's opportunity

Roger Casement in Germany

Roger Casement was born in Sandycove, Dublin, in 1864. He worked as a British diplomat and investigated human rights violations in the Congo and Peru, for which he was knighted. When back in Ireland, he became interested in the Republican movement, in particular Arthur Griffith's Sinn Féin, the non-violent movement towards Irish Independence. Casement ended up helping Eoin MacNeill set up the Irish Volunteers in 1913. He helped organise the Howth gunrunning in 1914, which was great experience for his next task!

Casement travelled to Germany in late 1914 to arrange German support for Irish independence. He hoped for German troops, and maybe artillery and military advisers too. He also tried to recruit Irish prisoners of war (POWs) who'd been captured by the Germans while fighting for the British, but he could not convince them. Ultimately all the Germans had to offer was 20,000 captured Russian rifles, 10 machine guns and some ammunition.

Roger Casement negotiating with the Germans

1916 Off to a Bad Start

OH NEIN!!

S.S. LIBAU DISGUISED AS
NORWEGIAN SHIP 'AUD'

A s Easter week approached, the weapons aboard the German ship SS 'Libau', which was disguised as a Norwegian vessel and called 'Aud', headed towards Ireland. Casement thought they weren't enough and travelled ahead aboard a submarine to warn MacNeill that any rising would be a disaster. He landed in Tralee Bay in the early hours of Good Friday, but was soon captured by British forces and charged with treason, sabotage and espionage against the Crown. The 'Libau' was intercepted by the British Navy and the weapons never made it.

HANDS UP!!

NOW WAS NOT A GOOD TIME FOR MY MALARIA TO FLARE UP!!

Casement caught under
the weather

NO PARADES!

Irish Volunteer Marches Cancelled

A SUDDEN ORDER.

The Easter manoeuvres of the Irish Volunteers, which were arranged to begin to-day, and of which the branches of the organisation in city and country were instructed last night, have been cancelled last night.

The following announcement was communicated to the Press last evening by the Staff of the Volunteers:—

April 22, 1916.

Owing to the very critical position, all orders given to Irish Volunteers for tomorrow, Easter Sunday, are hereby rescinded, and no parades, marches, or other movements of Irish Volunteers will take place. Each individual Volunteer will obey this order strictly in every particular.

EOIN MACNEILL,
Chief of Staff,
Irish Volunteers

MacNeill's countermanding order

That same week, Eoin MacNeill found out about the plans for the Rising. He thought it was crazy for an amateur force to fight against the well-oiled, well-trained British Army. He was shown a letter, allegedly from Dublin Castle, threatening the arrest of all the Irish Volunteer leaders.

On Good Friday, Patrick Pearse and Seán Mac Diarmada convinced him that German aid was coming, which initially worked. That same day, the IRB kidnapped Bulmer Hobson, who was opposed to the Rising. They held him at gunpoint at a house in Phibsborough until the Rising could get under way. Upon hearing this and the news of the disastrous capture of the German arms, MacNeill sent out a countermanding order. No Volunteers were to do anything on Easter Sunday! No marches! No manoeuvres! No parades! Word spread across the country fast, and the Rising was off, or so he thought ...

Bulmer Hobson kidnapped in Cabra

29

1916 Last-Minute Changes

The Military Council had an emergency meeting on Easter Sunday in Liberty Hall to discuss the shambles of a situation. MacNeill's countermanding order threw a complete spanner in the works. Volunteers across the country thought it was all called off. The Military Council decided that the Rising would take place the following day, Easter Monday, at noon. Because they couldn't spread this message around the country fast enough at such short notice, the Rising would be focused around Dublin with a few pockets of resistance elsewhere.

The Military Council meets one last time in Liberty Hall

Writing the Proclamation of Independence

The seven leaders, acting as the Provisional Government of the Irish Republic, drafted up and signed the Proclamation of Independence, a document outlining the Republic that they wanted to establish for Ireland. It guaranteed 'religious and civil liberty, equal rights and equal opportunities to all its citizens' and declaring 'its resolve to pursue the happiness and prosperity of the whole nation and of all its parts, cherishing all the children of the nation equally'.

They signed it and sent it to the printers for the big day. They had a busy week ahead!

The Proclamation of Independence and its signatories

PATRICK PEARSE

JAMES CONNOLLY

THOMAS CLARKE

POBLACHT NA H EIREANN.
THE PROVISIONAL GOVERNMENT
OF THE
IRISH REPUBLIC
TO THE PEOPLE OF IRELAND.

31

SEAN MAC DIARMADA

THOMAS MACDONAGH

ÉAMONN CEANNT

JOSEPH PLUNKETT

1916 The Rising

The unsuspecting public got on with enjoying the long weekend. Easter Monday was a sunny day and many had gone to the Irish Grand National horse race at Fairyhouse, outside Dublin. As the morning wore on, Irish Volunteers and Irish Citizen Army members gathered in their designated mustering

The Volunteers and Citizen Army gather in front of Liberty Hall

points around the city. Pearse and Connolly's forces gathered in front of Liberty Hall. Irish Volunteer Michael O'Rahilly, known as The O'Rahilly, had spent the weekend spreading MacNeill's countermanding order across Munster. When he heard it was happening anyway, he arrived in his motorcar saying 'I helped to wind up the clock. I might as well hear it strike!' Just before noon, 200 men and women marched up Lower Abbey Street and right onto Sackville Street to capture the General Post Office (GPO), which would be their headquarters.

YOU ARE MOST WELCOME!!

I HELPED TO WIND UP THE CLOCK! I MIGHT AS WELL HEAR IT STRIKE!!

The O'Rahilly arrives

The rebels barged into the GPO, guns ablaze, telling the civilians to leave. Not all of them took the rebels seriously but they cleared out nonetheless. The rebels raised the Irish tricolour above the GPO along with a green flag with 'Irish Republic' emblazoned in

Rebels charging the GPO on Sackville Street

white and orange letters. At 12.45 p.m., Pearse stepped out in front of the GPO and read aloud the Proclamation to a small and less-than-enthusiastic crowd. Clarke, Connolly, Plunkett and Mac Diarmada stood by him. When Pearse was finished, Connolly said to him 'Thank God we have lived to see this day!' Rebels were capturing buildings all across the city.

The Irish Republic flag flown above the GPO

ARE YOU SERIOUS, LOVE?

Many Dubliners were unimpressed

33

DUBLIN 1916
(NOT TO SCALE...)

1. The Magazine Fort
2. Marlborough Barracks
3. Islandbridge Barracks
4. Kilmainham Gaol
5. Richmond Barracks
6. The Royal Hospital
7. Kingsbridge Station
8. South Dublin Union
9. The Royal Barracks
10. The Mendicity Institution
11. North Dublin Union
12. Father Mathew Hall
13. The Four Courts
14. Marrowbone Lane Distillery
15. Williams & Woods Factory
16. Dublin Castle and City Hall
17. Jacob's Factory
18. Wellington Barracks
19. General Post Office
20. Liberty Hall
21. Trinity College
22. Royal College of Surgeons
23. St Stephen's Green
24. The Shelbourne Hotel
25. Harcourt Street Station
26. Portobello Barracks
27. Amiens Street Station
28. Westland Row Station
29. Boland's Mill
30. Mount Street Bridge
31. Beggars Bush Barracks

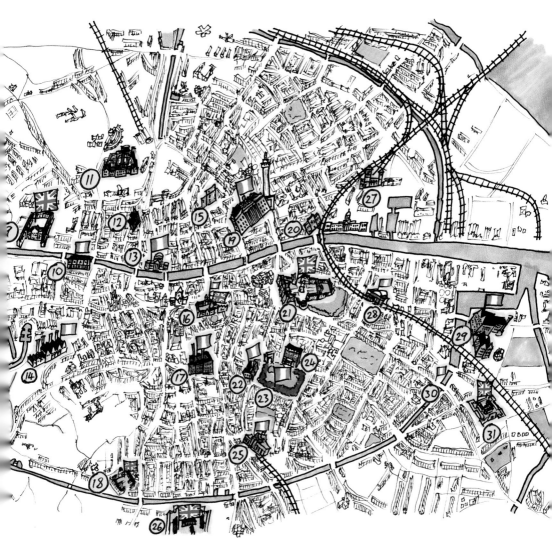

Buildings of the Rising

The GPO was chosen as the main HQ for the Rising as it was the main hub of telegraph communication in Dublin. The longer they could delay messages getting to Britain, the more hope the rebels had of strengthening their position. They sandbagged the doors and windows and got ready for a long siege. They barricaded the streets to stop the movement of people.

The first British response was a small cavalry charge from the Parnell Monument at the top of Sackville Street, but the rebels opened fire, killing four. Law and order quickly broke down and the poor people of Dublin started looting the shops.

The GPO captured

IRISHMEN AND IRISHWOMEN!! IN THE NAME OF GOD AND OF THE DEAD GENERATIONS FROM WHICH SHE RECEIVES HER OLD TRADITION OF NATIONHOOD, IRELAND, THROUGH US, SUMMONS HER CHILDREN TO HER FLAG AND STRIKES FOR HER FREEDOM!!

Pearse reading the Proclamation

LONG LIVE THE IRISH REPUBLIC... OR WHATEVER!

Many people began looting the shops

CHARGE!!!

INDEED OUR HORSES GIVE US A DISTINCT ADVANTAGE OVER THE MEN INSIDE THE G.P.O.!

36

The Magazine Fort over in the Phoenix Park was captured by a group of young rebels. It housed a cache of British ammunition and explosives. The rebels were to blow this up, signalling across the city the beginning of the Rising, but the fuses burnt out before they could blow it up properly.

The Magazine Fort

IT'S GONNA BLOW... ANY MINUTE NOW... JUST YOU WAIT...

UM... I MAY HAVE GOT THE FUSES WET... JUST SAYING...

Dublin Castle was the centre of British rule in Ireland. It was believed to be well guarded, but a small group of the Irish Citizen Army (ICA) travelled from Liberty Hall, led by theatre actor Seán Connolly. They shot an unarmed policeman, and British soldiers came out firing. The rebels retreated to the adjoining City Hall, not knowing there were actually very few soldiers stationed at the Castle, but they'd soon be reinforced. Seán Connolly was killed by a sniper, the first rebel to die in the Rising. City Hall would be overrun the following day. Senior officer Dr Kathleen Lynn led out the rebels in surrender. The Rising would last longer, though!

CITY HALL

DUBLIN CASTLE

PHEW!?

City Hall and Dublin Castle

YOU CAN GO HOME, LADIES.

ARREST US WITH THE REST OF THE SOLDIERS!

The arrest of Dr Kathleen Lynn

Ned Daly

Seán Heuston

The Four Courts

Most British Army barracks were outside the city centre. If the rebels could capture strategic buildings to block movement from these barracks, they could, theoretically, hold the city.

The 1st Battalion of the Irish Volunteers, under Edward ('Ned') Daly, mustered at Blackhall Street and occupied the Four Courts to control the River Liffey. They held areas as far as the North Dublin Union to stop troops coming from Marlborough Barracks and the Royal Barracks (Collins Barracks today). Cumann na mBan ran a makeshift hospital in Father Mathew Hall in this area. Limerick-born Ned Daly was the youngest leader of the Rising at the age of 25. His sister Kathleen was married to Tom Clarke.

Seán Heuston, a young Dubliner who was very involved in Fianna Éireann, led the 1st Battalion's D company to occupy the Mendicity Institution, a charity for the poor. It was also in view of Kingsbridge (now Heuston) Railway Station, where British reinforcements could arrive into the city.

The Mendicity Institution

Jacob's factory

NEED A HAND, LADS?

SURE! NO STEALING BISCUITS THOUGH!

John MacBride meets Thomas McDonagh and Michael O'Hanrahan

Thomas McDonagh was in charge of the 2nd Battalion at St Stephen's Green. Mayo-born IRB man John MacBride met them by chance on Grafton Street. The 47-year-old had kept out of the planning as he was known to British authorities. He offered his services and McDonagh gladly accepted. They moved to capture Jacob's biscuit factory (the National Archives today) on Bishop Street. This high building looked towards Rathmines and was chosen to hold up troops from Portobello Barracks. The Jacob's garrison didn't see much fighting in the Rising.

Michael Mallin, a socialist leader from Dublin, led some of the ICA to St Stephen's Green and there they dug trenches while Constance Markievicz oversaw the building of barricades along the streets. A civilian was shot while trying to grab a vehicle from the barricade. People were outraged at these rowdy, violent rebels taking the Green and ruining a good Easter Monday! By Tuesday evening, British soldiers had set up machine guns on the roof of the Shelbourne Hotel, making the trenches useless! Quickly the ICA had to retreat into the Royal College of Surgeons.

GEE, THESE TRENCHES WERE A GREAT IDEA!

Mallin and Markievicz under fire from the Shelbourne Hotel

Royal College of Surgeons

39

Éamon de Valera was born in New York in 1882 to an Irish mother and Spanish father. He was taken back to Ireland at the age of two, after his father died, and was raised by his grandmother in Limerick. He as a maths teacher and contemplated becoming a priest. His nickname was 'Dev'. He got involved in the Irish Volunteers and the IRB.

Éamon de Valera

The 3rd Battalion of Volunteers, with Dev as commandant, took over Boland's Mill by the Grand Canal Docks to control the approach into the city from Beggars Bush Barracks. They controlled the railway stations at Harcourt Street and Westland Row to prevent British reinforcements arriving from Kingstown (now Dún Laoghaire) Harbour.
Dev refused to let women fighters into Boland's Mill.

Boland's Mill

Éamonn Ceannt was commandant of the 4th Battalion at the South Dublin Union, the city's biggest workhouse for the poor. They would hold back British troops coming from Kilmainham Barracks and Richmond Barracks and their position overlooking the railway leading into Kingsbridge Station would hopefully let them slow down British reinforcements from Athlone and the Curragh.

Kingsbridge Station

His battalion saw fierce fighting coming from Kilmainham. Ceannt's forces under Limerick-born Con Colbert also occupied the Marrowbone Lane Distillery and stopped troops breaking through to Dublin Castle.

HOPEPULLY I DON'T GET SHOT!

THIS IS WHERE WE MAKE OUR STAND, CATHAL!

Eamon Ceannt and Cathal Brugha at the South Dublin Union

Con Colbert

The railways weren't captured, so British reinforcements were able to arrive from Athlone, the Curragh (via Kingsbridge Station) and Belfast (via Amiens Street Station).

LADS, YOUS BETTER NOT BE DRINKING THAT WHISKEY!

≡HICCUP≡

Barricade of barrels at Marrowbone Lane Distillery

1916 The British Response

British soldiers hold the barricades

1,000 TROOPS

Brigadier-General William Lowe

The element of surprise worked! The rebels had caught the British off guard. Rebel positions communicated via messengers, mostly young boys or women. Upon news of the rebellion reaching the Curragh military camp in Co. Kildare, Brigadier General William Lowe ordered a swift response and began sending troops to Dublin on Monday evening. Trinity College was chosen as a base for the army as it was large and in a very strong position. Early on Tuesday morning, Lowe arrived from the Curragh and assumed control of the British forces in Dublin. (A thing to remember about these 'British' soldiers is that most of the first to respond were Irishmen!)

Tuesday saw a strengthening of British positions around the city, building barricades of their own. The ICA was driven from St Stephen's Green into the Royal College of Surgeons, City Hall fell to the British and the British gunboat 'Helga' came up the Liffey and began shelling Boland's Mill.

IT'S NOT OVER TIL THE FAT LADY SINGS!

The gunboat 'Helga'

42

Francis Sheehy Skeffington

The looting continued and pacifist Francis Sheehy Skeffington was out on the streets to stop the looting. On Tuesday evening, as he walked to his Rathmines home, he was followed by hecklers, who shouted his nickname 'Skeffy!' At Portobello Bridge, Skeffington was arrested by British soldiers. Early on Wednesday, he was unjustly executed along with two journalists.

Thomas Ashe

Outside Dublin, Eoin MacNeill's countermanding order had had its effect, but there were pockets of rebellion. Rebels in north Co. Dublin, led by Thomas Ashe, began attacking RIC barracks and damaging railroads and telegraph lines.

In Cork, British forces moved to arrest prominent Irish Volunteers, including Thomas Kent. He had stayed at home but when authorities arrived at his house there ensued a three-hour gunfight. Kent was later arrested. In Galway, volunteers under Liam Mellows attempted to attack RIC barracks in Oranmore and Clarinbridge before moving across to the outskirts of Athenry. They would be chased by British forces as the week went on.

FOR ONCE, I HAD NOTHING TO DO WITH THIS!!

Thomas Kent

GALWAY WILL RISE TOO!!

Liam Mellows

1916 Reinforcements from England

Back in Dublin on Wednesday morning, the 'Helga' began shelling Liberty Hall, destroying it. British forces moved 18-pounder howitzer guns into position to begin shelling Sackville Street. British troops stayed back while the shelling commenced, giving the rebels nothing to shoot at.

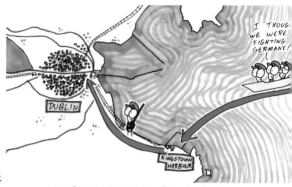

I THOUG WE WERE FIGHTING GERMANY!

DUBLIN

KINGSTOWN HARBOUR

Reinforcements arriving from England

British reinforcements from England had landed at Kingstown Harbour and they began to move towards the city. These soldiers were young and inexperienced. Some were still being shown how to work their Lee-Enfield rifles on the boat over. They began their march towards the city centre; half would go via Donnybrook, the other half would go via Northumberland Road and onto Mount Street Bridge, but the rebels were waiting for them.

18-pounder howitzer guns in front of Trinity College aimed at the GPO

44

The shelling of Liberty Hall

The Battle of Mount Street Bridge

A detachment of Volunteers from Boland's Mill hid in various buildings along Northumberland Road and around Mount Street Bridge. As the Sherwood Foresters walked past the RDS, the local Dubliners cheered them on. South Dublin was very Unionist and pro-British. As the army moved up Northumberland Road, they met heavy fire coming from the few rebels. They were walking into a kill zone. They took the whole day to push up to Mount Street Bridge, taking huge casualties along the way. They eventually captured some of the rebels while others either escaped or were killed. This handful of rebels managed to kill four officers and either kill or wound 216 soldiers. Mount Street Bridge was to be taken at all costs ... and it was!

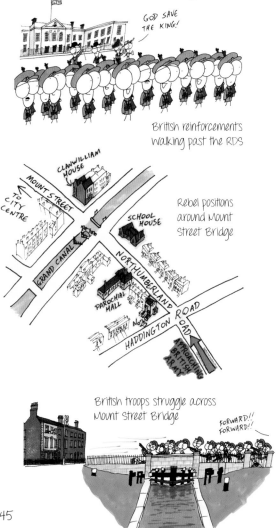

GOD SAVE THE KING!

British reinforcements walking past the RDS

Rebel positions around Mount Street Bridge

British troops struggle across Mount Street Bridge

FORWARD!! FORWARD!!

45

1916 The Rising Rages On

James Connolly broadcast a message in morse code: 'Irish Republic declared in Dublin today. Irish troops have captured city and are in full possession. Enemy cannot move in city. The whole country rising.' Word of the rebellion spread around the country and, indeed, the world. Rebels in Enniscorthy, Co. Wexford, rose up on the Thursday and captured the town! Like the United Irishmen of the 1798 Rebellion, rebels occupied Vinegar Hill.

The shelling of Sackville Street saw fires break out, which had developed into an inferno by the end of the day. Amidst the fighting, James Connolly was hit in the leg by a ricocheting bullet and was unable to walk for the rest of the Rising, but he still gave the orders! The rebels sang together 'The Soldier's Song', which would later become the Irish national anthem. British forces began closing in on rebel positions. Their supplies were seemingly infinite compared to the seriously limited resources of the rebels.

IRISH REPUBLIC DECLARED IN DUBLIN TODAY

Morse code transmission from Sackville Street to the world

LOOKS LIKE WE'RE BACK ON, LADS!!

Rebels in Enniscorthy

WE'VE NOTHING TO SHOOT AT!!

Shelling on Sackville Street

YOU REBEL SCUM!

I'M NOT A REBEL! I'M JUST ANNOYED — YOU POKED A HOLE IN MY BLEEDIN' WALL!!!

British soldiers burrowing through North King Street

Connolly hit by a ricocheting bullet

Fighting was fierce along North King Street. British soldiers broke into civilian houses and burrowed their way through the walls to stay out of the line of fire in the streets. By Saturday, 15 civilians had been murdered, accused of being rebels.

Fighting intensified at the South Dublin Union. Éamonn Ceannt's second in command, Cathal Brugha, was severely wounded, sustaining up to 25 wounds. He was left for dead in a retreat but he was later found alive, revolver in hand, lying in his own blood, singing 'God Save Ireland'.

"GOD SAVE IRELAND!" SAID THE HEROES; "GOD SAVE IRELAND" SAID THEY ALL.

Cathal Brugha left for dead

1916 The British Close In

By Friday, Sackville Street was ablaze and things were looking more and more hopeless for the rebels.

Meanwhile in Ashbourne, Co. Meath, the Fingal Volunteers under Thomas Ashe had attacked an RIC barracks. The arrival of RIC reinforcements resulted in the Battle of Ashbourne, a five-hour gunfight.

Sackville Street ablaze

Battle of Ashbourne

General Sir John Maxwell was sent from London to take charge of the British forces. He arrived on the Friday and acted as the military governor, looking to quell this rebellion with an iron fist. The British forces at this point numbered nearly 16,000. He continued the shelling of rebel-held buildings across Dublin.

Sir John Maxwell

48

Inside the GPO

With Sackville Street a blazing inferno, it was too dangerous to remain at the GPO. Pearse and the rebels decided to make for the Williams & Woods Factory on Kings Inn Street, then head west to meet Ned Daly's battalion at the Four Courts and fight their way north out of the city.

The rebels fled towards Moore Street but British machine guns cut down many of them, including The O'Rahilly, the only Volunteer leader to be killed in the fighting. He would lie dying in the street for the next few days.

The O'Rahilly dying

A young Cork-born Volunteer, Michael Collins, helped with the evacuation. Connolly was carried on a stretcher and the rebels eventually broke their way into the buildings of Moore Street. They burrowed through the walls and settled in and around 16 Moore Street to regroup.

The rebels burrowing through Moore Street

49

1916 Surrender

The death toll of the Rising continued to grow as the days went by, especially amongst civilians caught in the crossfire. Most civilian deaths were caused by British soldiers, through artillery bombardment, the use of heavy machine guns in narrow streets and the inability of the British to discern between rebels and civilians. People fleeing their homes in Moore Street were gunned down. This had to stop!

On Saturday the leaders in Moore Street decided to seek surrender terms to stop the civilian slaughter. Cumann na mBan member Elizabeth O'Farrell, who had been tending to the wounded Connolly, was sent out with a white flag to approach the British barricade at the top of Moore Street. She was brought to General William Lowe, who offered only unconditional surrender. She returned with Pearse who formally surrendered to Lowe on Great Britain (now Parnell) Street.

I ACCEPT YOUR OFFER OF UNCONDITION... SURRENDER.

GENERAL LOWE

SERIOUSLY? NOW IS THE TIME YOU CHOOSE TO LIGHT A CIGARETTE?

Patrick Pearse surrendering to General Lowe

Elizabeth O'Farrell

Dublin in ruins

O'Farrell and a priest, Father Augustine, carefully travelled across the city with the surrender order and, one by one, the rebels stood down. Some British authorities didn't know what to do with the women who were involved. Some were allowed to go home, some insisted on being arrested with their brothers in arms. As the rebels were rounded up and marched through the streets, they were heckled, spat on and jeered at by

Elizabeth O'Farrell and Fr Augustine Hayden walking through Dublin with the surrender order

Dubliners, who believed this death and destruction was their fault! Most of the rebels were held in the yard of the Rotunda Hospital off the top of Sackville Street. Tom Clarke and Ned Daly were mocked and abused in front of their comrades by Captain Percival Lea-Wilson. Young Michael Collins witnessed all this, and he would not forget it.

FENIAN SWINE!

Captain Percival Lea-Wilson abusing Tom Clarke

1916 Summary Justice

A RATHER CUNNING PLAN SIR!

WE WILL EXECUTE THESE REBEL SCUM!

In all, 485 people died in the Rising: 82 rebels, 126 British forces (a third of whom were Irishmen), 17 policemen and 260 civilians. Among these were 38 children under 16, the youngest being two-year-old Christina Caffrey.

Blackader and Maxwell

General Maxwell was not going to waste time in dealing out justice towards these rebels and enemies of the Empire. The courts martial were held at Richmond Barracks in secret. They were presided over by General Charles Blackader and two other army officers; these trials were not for the public! The rebels had surrendered on the Saturday and the courts martial began the following Monday. Tom Clarke didn't speak a word throughout his trial. Patrick Pearse said in his trial, 'If you strike us down now, we will rise again and renew the fight! You cannot conquer Ireland. You cannot extinguish the Irish passion for freedom. If our deed has not been sufficient to win freedom for Ireland, then our children will win it by a better deed.'

GERMANY IS NO MORE TO ME THAN ENGLAND IS!

Pearse's court martial

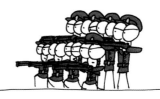

Pearse, Clarke and McDonagh were executed separately on the first day, 3 May

Pearse had confirmed in a letter to his mother that he had been awaiting German support, Britain's enemy. The letter, along with his actions in Easter week, sealed his fate. Some believe this was Pearse's plan all along; a blood sacrifice to inspire generations of Irish Republicans. Pearse was executed by firing squad the next day, 3 May, along with Tom Clarke and Thomas McDonagh in Kilmainham Gaol. The trials and executions would come swift and hard.

On 4 May, Ned Daly, Joseph Plunkett, Patrick Pearse's brother, Willie Pearse, and McDonagh's second in command, Michael O'Hanrahan, were executed. Plunkett had been allowed to marry his fiancée, Grace Gifford, in the gaol. Willie had little to do with the command, but his connection to Patrick, whom he'd fought beside in the GPO, was enough.

TILL DEATH DO US PART...

Grace Gifford marrying Joseph Plunkett

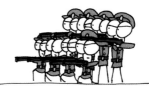

Joseph Plunkett, Ned Daly, Willie Pearse and Michael O'Hanrahan were executed on 4 May

53

On 5 May, John MacBride was executed. When offered a blindfold, MacBride said, 'I have looked down the muzzles of too many guns in the South African war to fear death and now please carry out your sentence,' and he faced the firing squad without a blindfold.

John MacBride was executed on 5 May

Monday 8 May saw the executions of Éamonn Ceannt, Michael Mallin, Con Colbert and Seán Heuston. Meanwhile in Cork, Thomas Kent, who'd been arrested during the week, was executed on 9 May.

Con Colbert, Seán Heuston, Michael Mallin and Éamonn Ceannt were executed on 8 May

General Maxwell had had 3,400 Republican sympathisers arrested (twice as many as had been involved in the Rising) and 97 men and 1 woman were sentenced to death. While many were released, 1,841 people were interned in Wales and England.

By 12 May, only two of the signatories of the Proclamation remained: Séan Mac Diarmada and James Connolly. Connolly was being held in Dublin Castle because of his gangrenous leg. He was brought to Kilmainham Gaol, strapped to a chair and put before the firing squad. Connolly, a long-time atheist, said to his firing squad: 'I will say a prayer for all men who do their duty according to the lights.' MacDiarmada was executed that day, too.

Seán Mac Diarmada (above) and James Connolly (left) were the last to be executed on 12 May

HEY! I'M NOT A SINN FÉINER!!

WELL YOU LOOK LIKE ONE!

The public were not happy with the mass arrests that followed the Rising

54

1916 The Dust Settles

As news of the executions spread, people began to question such justice. Patrick Pearse was executed a week and a day after he'd read the Proclamation in front of the GPO. It was all happening so quickly. Because the courts martial were held in private, people began to think these men were being executed in cold blood. Outrage was growing.

The British Prime Minister himself, Herbert Asquith, arrived in Dublin on the day Mac Diarmada and Connolly were shot. He urged Maxwell to stop the executions. He was making martyrs out of them. The executions stopped, letting Constance Markievicz, William T. Cosgrave and Éamon de Valera off the hook. Roger Casement, however, would later be tried and hanged in London, on 3 August, for his involvement in the German gun smuggling.

THEY KILLED ANOTHER ONE?

THEY MUST'VE DIED FOR SOMETHING.

Public opinion began to turn sympathetic towards the executed leaders

I THOUGHT I WAS TEACHING THEM A LESSON!

YOU'RE MAKING MARTYRS OF THEM!!

British Prime Minister H. H. Asquith and Maxwell

GENTLEMEN, I THINK WE MAY BE OFF THE HOOK!

PHEW!

Countess Markievicz, Éamon de Valera and W. T. Cosgrave avoided execution

Roger Casement

1916 Training in Jail

Michael Collins

Michael Collins was born in 1890 in Sam's Cross, near Clonakilty, Co. Cork. He grew up in a proudly Republican family. His fiery, passionate and precocious personality earned him the nickname 'The Big Fellah'. He moved to London in his late teenage years and worked as a messenger for a stockbroker. He got involved in the London GAA and was brought into the IRB by GAA man Sam Maguire. He got involved in the Easter Rising, working as Joseph Plunkett's personal assistant in the GPO. After the rebels were rounded up, Collins and many others were taken to Frongoch internment camp in Wales. It was there that Collins emerged as a natural leader, training the men in guerrilla warfare. Tactics such as ambushes, hit-and-run attacks, sabotage and raids allowed a smaller, less-well-equipped fighting force to stand a chance against the might of the British Army. 'Guerrilla' comes from the Spanish word for 'little war'. This time in prison allowed Collins to network with other Republicans from all over Ireland and prepare them for the next time!

RIGHT, LADS! LET'S GET THIS TRAINING STARTED!!

Frongoch Prison, Wales

1916-1917 Mustering Public

I AM FREE FROM BRITISH IMPRISONMENT, AND FREE OF MY MOUSTACHE!

YAY!!

Dev returns to a hero's welcome

De Valera and the other leaders were doing time in English jails but pressure was growing on the British government. Sympathy for the Republicans was steadily on the rise in Ireland. In December 1916, the prisoners in Frongoch were released. They helped stir up more sympathy back home. Dubliner Joseph McGuinness was elected as a Member of Parliament for South Longford in a 1917 by-election, despite being in jail in England.

PUT HIM IN, TO GET HIM OUT!!

JOSEPH McGUINNESS

Collins campaigning for Joseph McGuinness who was still in prison

The new British Prime Minister, David Lloyd George, announced an amnesty for the political prisoners. Dev and the other released prisoners were given a hero's welcome in Ireland. The people looked to them for new leadership. Many believed it was Sinn Féin who'd started The Rising, so the newly released prisoners joined that party and reorganised Arthur Griffith's original vision to match the Republican agenda, with Dev as President.

THEY HAVE BRANDED ME A CRIMINAL. EVEN THOUGH IF I DIE, I DIE IN A GOOD CAUSE.

Thomas Ashe, the leader of the Rising rebels in north Dublin, was re-arrested and imprisoned for speaking out against the British. He and others went on hunger strike, refusing to eat, to demand status as POWs, rather than as petty criminals. Ashe died on hunger strike, winning POW status for others. His funeral was another rousing call to the Republicans.

1917-1918 The Conscription

NOT A HOPE!!

The war was still raging in Europe and because of the horror stories coming back from the trenches and a high death rate amongst Irish regiments, it was more and more difficult to find new recruits. The British government wanted to bring in conscription, forcing people into the army, but that went down like a lead balloon in Ireland! Huge opposition from Sinn Féin, the Labour Party, trade unions and the Catholic Church united the people against British conscription.

It didn't help in May 1918 when British authorities arrested over 70 leading members of Sinn Féin in one night for alleged links with Germany. The leaders had received a tip-off about the arrest. Some, such as Éamon de Valera, chose to be arrested and use it as propaganda for more public outrage; others, like Michael Collins, chose to remain free. Collins was in favour of the more militant, direct IRB method towards fighting the British. Ultimately, conscription didn't happen in Ireland and the Great War ended in November, but the people had had enough.

THE IRISH PEOPLE WILL NOT BE IMPRESSED!

SHUT UP! YOU'LL NEVER AMOUNT TO ANYTHING WHERE YOU'RE GOING!

Dev arrested again

1918 The 1918 General Election

The 1918 General Election was a game changer for Ireland. The Labour Party chose not to contest the election so as not to split the Irish vote: a united front was needed. A vote for Sinn Féin was a vote for independence. They won a huge victory, winning 73 out of 105 seats, the majority of the constituencies across Ireland (except the predominantly Unionist North). Some had voted for the Irish Parliamentary Party, still believing in Home Rule, but for the majority, that ship had sailed. They wanted independence and Sinn Féin were to deliver it!

THE LABOUR PARTY ARE GONNA SIT THIS ONE OUT!

Thomas Johnson, leader of the Irish Labour Party

BRITISH PARLIAMENT ELECTION RESULTS

- SINN FÉIN
- IRISH UNIONISTS
- IRISH PARLIAMENTARY PARTY
- LABOUR UNIONISTS

1918 general election

1919 The First Dáil

Mansion House, Dublin

WE DECLARE INDEPENDENCE!!

Cathal Brugha, temporary President of Dáil Éireann

On 21 January 1919, those elected Sinn Féin officials who weren't in prison or on the run met in the Mansion House in Dublin to form the First Dáil Éireann (Parliament of Ireland). Even though these elected officials were Members of the British Parliament, and had their seats to take in Westminster, they chose to establish the new parliament in Dublin and give the people what they wanted: an Independent Ireland. The members were now Teachtaí Dála, or TDs, members of Dáil Éireann. Cathal Brugha was elected temporary President of Dáil Éireann as Dev was still in jail. They declared Ireland's independence, presented a provisional constitution, outlined how the Republic was going to be run and urged the rest of the world to recognise their independence.

Britain was not impressed.

1919 The War of Independence Begins

The Royal Irish Constabulary, the police force in Ireland

Meanwhile, on the same day as the First Dáil was meeting, Irish Volunteers, including Seán Treacy and Dan Breen, acting on their own, without Dáil consent, launched an ambush at Soloheadbeg, Co. Tipperary. They killed two RIC policemen and stole a consignment of gelignite explosives. The first shots of the Irish War of Independence had been fired!

Irish Volunteers across the country were told that British forces were to be treated as an invading army, and with deadly force, if necessary. Volunteers raided RIC barracks across the country, stealing better weaponry as they went. The war was on!

Soloheadbeg Ambush

1919 Jailbreak

Harry Boland

Dubliner Harry Boland was involved with the IRB from a young enough age. He fought in the Easter Rising and was elected as a TD in 1918. He was good friends with Michael Collins and together they made a great team.

Éamon de Valera was being held in Lincoln Prison, England. Collins and Boland planned a daring escape for him. The plans were sung to Dev in Irish over the prison walls. Dev was a devout Catholic

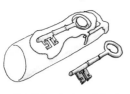
Candle impression of the key used to make a copy

and during his time in the prison church, he was able to make a sneaky impression of the chaplain's master key on a wax candle. He threw the candle over the wall for the Irish agents to pick up. From it, they made copies of the key, smuggled one back into Dev and took the other to the back gate in February 1919.

Irish girls distracted the prison guards while Dev and two other Sin Féiners, Seán McGarry and Seán Milroy, made their way to the back to meet Collins and Boland. Despite Collins' key breaking in the lock, they managed to open the door and escape, with Dev disguised in a big fur coat!

NO WORRIES, THE GUARDS ARE BUSY!!

The back gate of Lincoln Prison

He returned to Ireland and became President of the Dáil at their next meeting.

1919 G-men

MY JOB'S ABOUT TO GET A LOT WORSE!!

Member of the Dublin Metropolitan Police

Intelligence — what Britain knew about Republicans — was a major part of this war. The Dublin Metropolitan Police (DMP) had a special division of plain-clothes policemen, the G Division. These 'G-men' would follow known Sinn Féin members and other undesirables around Dublin, tracking their movements and activities. The British were well informed.

Michael Collins was Director of Intelligence for the Volunteers and had already been setting up all sorts of weapons-smuggling operations to arm them. He established communication and intelligence networks of his own, through railway, postal, telephone and telegraph workers in Ireland and England. Kildare man Eamon 'Ned' Broy was a detective for the DMP but also worked as a double agent for Michael Collins. He was able to tell Collins how the whole police system operated and supplied Collins with copied files of what the G-men knew. In April 1919, Broy snuck Collins into the DMP Detective Headquarters on Brunswick Street (now Pearse Street) and allowed him to spend the night looking through their files. This was vital to the survival of the Republicans.

GOOD EVENING! MR. BROY.

JOHN GRACE — I PRESUME...

Collins meeting Ned Broy under the name John Grace

1919 The Limerick Soviet

A bread mill in the Limerick Soviet

Money printed in the Limerick Soviet

While Nationalism was the big thing in Ireland at that time, so too was socialism. In 1917, the people of Russia had a revolution and in 1918 they established the Soviet Russian Republic, a socialist state where farmland and industry was owned and run by the government, with everyone earning an equal share of the money. The idea of socialism was sweeping across Europe, including Ireland. After an attempted prisoner rescue by Irish Volunteers in Limerick, the city of Limerick was declared a 'Special Military Area'. People

The Hammer & Sickle was the symbol of socialism - hammer for the industry worker, sickle for the farm worker

needed special permits from the RIC to enter. In response, the Limerick Trades and Labour Council called a general strike and declared the Limerick Soviet. For two weeks in April 1919, the people of Limerick printed their own money, controlled food prices and printed their own newspapers. The Sinn Féin mayor, Alphonsus O'Mara, and Catholic bishop Dennis Hallinan ultimately called for the strike to end and with it ended the Limerick Soviet.

The word 'Soviet' comes from the Russian word for 'council'.

1919-1923 Socialism in Ireland

Socialism, Republicanism and Imperialism

Over the next few years, during the War of Independence and later the Civil War, many workers across the country seized their own factories, foundries, mills and mines, raising the red flag of socialism and taking control back for the working people. In some ways, this was as much a threat, if not more, to Britain than the Nationalists. The last thing Britain needed was these socialist ideas spreading to English cities and crumbling the Empire from within. Most of these protests were either suppressed or appeased by both British and Irish Nationalist forces.

65

1919 International Outreach

A t the end of the Great War, all the world leaders met in Paris to put together what would become the Treaty of Versailles. Dublin TD Seán T. O'Kelly was in Paris to try and get Ireland internationally recognised as an independent republic. He was particularly interested in getting some time with United States President Woodrow Wilson but to no avail. De Valera decided to travel to the United States himself. He

Seán T. O'Kelly

THE THINGS WE MUST DO FOR POLITICS...

and others, including Harry Boland, left in June 1919.

Dev went to gain support from the American people, raise money for their cause and seek official recognition from the US. He toured the US, talking to many Irish-American groups. He managed to raise around $5.5m for the Republican cause. Dev would stay in America for 18 months, leaving effective command of the war to Michael Collins, who was the Minister for Finance at the time. Arthur Griffith was acting President of the Dáil in Dev's absence.

Signing of the Treaty of Versailles

United States President Woodrow Wilson

Dev wearing a traditional Native American headdress while in America

US and Irish flags

1919 The Republic Ignores the Empire

While Dev was abroad, the Dáil set up the Dáil courts, to replace the British legal system. Small courts were set up around the country and Irish Volunteers, clergymen or Sinn Féin figures would be the judges. Women were eligible to be judges in this system.

At the same time, Michael Collins was made president of the IRB. He was overseeing the war across Ireland. Tipperary, in particular, saw many conflicts between the Volunteers and British operatives. Indeed, Sinn Féin, Conradh na Gaeilge, Cumann na mBan and the Irish Volunteers were made illegal in Tipperary, not that that would stop them!

Collins knew he needed to get rough...er.

Dáil Courts

Volunteers shooting an RIC constable in Thurles

Banned organisations

1919 The Squad

Some of Collins' assassination squad

While Sinn Féin in the Dáil were opting for a non-violent approach towards the DMP through mild intimidation, persuasion and boycotting, Michael Collins believed this wasn't enough. He had Dublin IRA man Dick McKee assemble a group of men who would become The Squad, or The Twelve Apostles. These men would be a guerrilla assassination squad who targeted G-men and other civil servants loyal to the Crown. Collins wanted to make opposing the Irish Republic a more and more undesirable task.

The first assassination was of G-man Detective Sergeant Patrick Smith in Drumcondra, and many more were to follow. The Squad would work in small numbers, emerging from a crowd, firing their shots and disappearing again. Collins knew they couldn't match the might of the British Army so he ran his war in a way that worked.

G-Man Patrick Smith found by his son outside his house.

68

1919 The Irish Republican Army

Some in the Dáil worried that the Irish Volunteers had too much independence and that they should be answerable to the government of the Irish Republic. In August 1919, an oath of allegiance was introduced and Volunteers began to pledge themselves to the Irish Republic. The Irish Volunteers were no more: they would now be the Irish Republican Army (IRA). Waterford man Richard Mulcahy became their chief of staff.

I'LL KEEP THE BOYS IN LINE!

Richard Mulcahy

The attacks on British forces would continue but retaliation was coming! After IRA volunteers under Liam Lynch attacked a company of British troops in Fermoy in September, killing one and capturing some rifles, 200 British troops looted and burned businesses in Fermoy in revenge for the attack. These reprisals would become a staple of the British response.

— THAT'LL TEACH 'EM!!

The burning of Fermoy

The badge of the armed forces of the Irish Republic, originally used by the Volunteers

The Dáil began producing 'The Irish Bulletin', a publication to communicate with the world and give them the Irish Republic's view on things.

1919 Can Home Rule Still Work?

British Prime Minister David Lloyd George

I STILL DON'T KNOW WHY WE CAN'T JUST BRING IN MARTIAL LAW AND SORT OUT THOSE PESKY REBELS!

Sir John French, Lord Lieutenant of Ireland

Meanwhile, Prime Minister David Lloyd George outlawed Dáil Éireann. The British government continued to explore the possibility of Home Rule with two parliaments, one in Dublin, one in Belfast. Sir John French, the Lord Lieutenant of Ireland, believed that Home Rule could still work. He didn't believe that Sinn Féin had much public support (he'd been responsible for the mass arrests in 1918). The IRA tried to assassinate him while he was on his way home to the Viceregal Lodge (now Áras an Uachtaráin) in the Phoenix Park, Dublin. The IRA set up a barricade to block French's motorcade and opened fire on the cars. They also threw grenades but failed to kill French. One IRA man was killed, and one wounded, along with two policemen and a driver.

As 1919 came to a close, worse was yet to come!

I'M PRETTY SURE THEY THINK I'M IN THAT SECOND CAR!

Assassination attempt on Sir John French in Phoenix Park

1920 The Black and Tans

WE WILL FIGHT IN THE FIELDS AND IN THE STREETS, WE SHALL FIGHT IN THE HILLS! WE SHALL NEVER SURRENDER! HMMM... I SHOULD WRITE THAT DOWN...

Winston Churchill, Secretary of State for War

The first half of 1920 saw the IRA actively targeting many RIC barracks around the country. In counties Cork, Waterford, Tipperary, Monaghan, barracks were burnt, in an attempt to destroy the infrastructure of British authorities. The British Secretary of State for War, Winston Churchill, had assembled a team of law enforcers, mainly veterans of the Great War. Many were eager to get a job after the war so the ranks were filled easily. There were so many recruits that there weren't enough proper uniforms to go around so they ended up with a mix of khaki British Army gear and the dark green RIC gear, which looked black. This uniform gave the RIC Special Reserve the infamous nickname 'The Black and Tans'.

The Black and Tans arrived in Ireland in March and they were vicious and brutal. They were more soldiers than police, and they would often take reprisals for IRA attacks out on civilians. Tuam, Balbriggan, Thurles and many other towns would burn before the end of 1920.

The Black and Tans

Burning of Galway

71

1920 The Divided North

YAY, IRISH INDEPENDENCE!

The Guild Hall, Derry/Londonderry

WHAT'S YOUR SURNAME? WHERE DID YOU GO TO SCHOOL? WHAT'S THE LAST LINE OF THE LORD'S PRAYER???

Religion checkpoint on the Carlisle Bridge in Derry/Londonderry

In Ulster, the deep-rooted religious and political divides were stronger than ever. Unionists in Derry had lost control of the Londonderry Corporation (the ruling council) to Irish Nationalists in the elections. IRA attacks on RIC barracks increased across the province. The Ulster Volunteers had a job to do!

Throughout April and May, tensions between Nationalists and Unionists turned into riots and violence. The Ulster Volunteers set up checkpoints on Carlisle (now Craigavon) Bridge and harassed Catholics. In June, many Catholics were driven out of the Waterside of Derry and an attack on the Bogside, a predominantly Catholic area, was made by the Ulster Volunteers and the British Army. By July, Catholics and Protestants were being forced out of their homes and up to 40 people were killed!

At that same time in Belfast, Loyalists forced over 7,000 Catholic workers out of their jobs in the shipyards. In the riots that followed, 22 people were killed. There would be no surrender!

YOUS ARE THE REASON THE TITANIC SANK!!

The shipyards of Belfast

1920 Frustrating the Empire

THIS IS FOR 1916!!

Assassination of Percival Lea-Wilson

The British war effort was hampered in many ways. Dublin dock workers and Irish rail workers refused to carry British war materials or troops. Michael Collins' men had hunted for Percival Lea-Wilson, the man who'd abused leaders of the Rising. The IRA tracked him down and shot him in Gorey, Co. Wexford.

EH... SORRY LADS, NOT TODAY...

YOU SURE ABOUT THAT?

Collins' campaign of G-men assassinations had damaged the British intelligence network. They had to bring in outside intelligence agents, a crack team of former British Army officers, later referred to as the Cairo Gang.

Railway protests

Once the Dáil courts were set up, Irish people began refusing to take part in the British courts, bringing the justice system to a standstill. Many RIC policemen retired or resigned, frustrated with the lack of justice. Many who stayed felt they had to deal their own justice.

The Cairo Gang

Auxiliary Division

At this time, the RIC was gaining even more reinforcement from the Auxiliary Division, or simply the Auxiliaries. They were a force similar to the Black and Tans, known for their brutality towards the Irish.

73

1920 Hunger Strikers

WE'RE PRISONER OF WAR, NOT CRIMINALS!

IT IS NOT THOSE WHO CAN INFLICT THE MOST, BUT THOSE THAT CAN SUFFER THE MOST WHO WILL CONQUER.

Terence MacSwiney on hunger strike

The war had allowed British authorities to introduce internment without trial so suspected IRA members or sympathisers were thrown in jail unjustly. In April 1920, prisoners in Mountjoy went on hunger strike, demanding political status. Many were released, which lessened the threat of internment. August, however, would see a controversial turn of events.

Prisoners in Cork went on hunger strike. Terence MacSwiney was Lord Mayor of Cork and an elected Sinn Féiner. He was arrested and imprisoned. He joined the hunger strike as soon as he arrived. Michael Fitzgerald would die in October after 67 days. MacSwiney was transferred to Brixton jail in England but he continued his hunger strike. After 74 days on hunger strike, he died. Joseph Murphy would die on the same day, after 76 days. Arthur Griffith called a halt to the hunger strike and the other eight survived. MacSwiney's hunger strike and death brought the Irish struggle international attention. The likes of USA, France, Germany and Australia looked on in disbelief. Ireland was bleeding.

Mountjoy Prison along the Royal Canal, Dublin

WHAT IS GOING ON OVER THERE?

International attention to the hunger strikes

1920 Tit for Tat

As the summer of 1920 raged on, attacks from both sides kept coming. RIC men were shot, the Tans took it out on the public and burnt Sinn Féin offices and halls. People connected to the British system were shot on the streets by the IRA.

The Cairo Gang continued their campaign on Sinn Féiners. TDs had each received a note: 'An eye for an eye, a tooth for a tooth. Therefore, a life for a life.' It was that kind of war: murders and reprisals.

In September, Peter Burke, the Head Constable of the RIC, was shot by the IRA in Balbriggan, Co. Dublin. The Black and Tans burned 54 businesses in Balbriggan and killed two suspected IRA men. But as autumn turned into winter, the most infamous reprisal occurred.

An eye for an eye,
A tooth for a tooth.
Therefore,
a life for a life.

A letter of warning

IRA men after another assassination

Burning of Balbriggan

1920 Bloody Sunday

Dublin Castle

I'M YOUR MAN IN THE CASTLE!

David Neligan

Collins' people had been gathering information about the Cairo Gang: who they were, places they frequented and where they lived. Limerick man David Neligan was Collins' inside man in Dublin Castle and supplied a lot of information. Dick McKee and Peadar Clancy brought the information together and, on 21 November, under the command of Michael Collins and Richard Mulcahy, The Squad and other IRA members were dispersed across Dublin with the names and addresses of British operatives, including many of the Cairo Gang. Most of the targets were in the south inner city.

At 9 a.m., they carried out a coordinated attack on their targets, executing 13 British operatives of various positions and wounding two others. Two civilians were killed and another was wounded, as well as one IRA man, Frank Teeling, who was captured.

Hit list

Auxies opening fire at the football match in Croke Park

The British response was swift and brutal. In the afternoon, the Auxiliaries moved on Croke Park where a Gaelic football match between Dublin and Tipperary was being played. Shots were fired and the crowd panicked. Some soldiers fired into the fleeing crowd. Twelve people were killed by British guns, another two were trampled in the stampede. Football player Michael Hogan was shot on the pitch; the Hogan Stand in Croke Park is named after him. The youngest killed that day was an 11-year-old boy.

Dick McKee, Peadar Clancy and Conor Clune were shot in Dublin Castle that night.

This infamous day would become known as Bloody Sunday unfortunately, it wouldn't be the only Bloody Sunday in Irish history.

An armoured car causing more panic outside Croke Park

ALL THESE DARK UNIFORMS; IT'S ALMOST AS IF WE'RE ACTIVELY TRYING TO LOOK SINISTER!

Ulster Special Constabulary

Two days after Bloody Sunday, Sinn Féin leaders Eoin MacNeill and Arthur Griffith were arrested. Martial law spread across the country. The British Army was in charge and could execute their prisoners! In Ulster, the Ulster Special Constabulary (part of which would later commonly be known as the B-Specials) were formed as a more militaristic backup for the RIC, made up almost entirely of Protestants. In retaliation for an IRA assault on an RIC barracks in Camlough, Co. Armagh, the Ulster Special Constabulary burnt buildings in Camlough.

In December, after an IRA attack on Auxiliaries in Cork, British authorities set fire to the centre of Cork city. The fire raged, destroying houses, businesses, City Hall and Carnegie Library. Fire brigades were delayed by intimidation from the Black and Tans. Civilians were shot at. It was chaos! Two IRA men were shot dead and a woman died of a heart attack when the Auxiliaries burst into her home.

The Burning of Cork

After the Burning of Cork, the Bishop of Cork Daniel Cohalan threatened excommunication to those organising ambushes and murders. At this time Éamon de Valera returned from America to a country at war.

DOWN WITH THAT SORT OF THING!

Meanwhile in Westminster, just before Christmas, the Government of Ireland Act 1920 came into law. Because the Sinn Féin representatives hadn't taken their places in Westminster, the Act was very out-of-touch with the developments in Ireland. It proposed that two parliaments be set up. Because of the strong Unionist presence in the six north-eastern counties, the parliament in Belfast would control these counties, which became Northern Ireland. The Dublin parliament would control the other 26 counties, becoming Southern Ireland. Both would remain part of the United Kingdom but Ireland itself was now divided. British military leaders believed the violence would last only a few more months. Of course, at this stage, many Irish people were past the point of no return when it came to the British Empire.

I'M BACK! WHAT DID I MISS??

Dev back from America

Bishop Daniel Cohalan

WELL THIS FEELS ISOLATING...

NORTHERN IRELAND

SOUTHERN IRELAND

The partition of the island

1921 Death to Informants

By 1921, the IRA were professionals at ambush and execution. Around the country, they would travel in flying columns, guerrilla groups ready to attack. They could hide from authorities in friendly houses or hideouts around the countryside.

BAH!

IRA members took rest wherever they could

In January in Cork, British authorities were tipped off about an IRA ambush in Dripsey by a local elderly widow, Mary Lindsay, resulting in the death of seven IRA men. Mrs Lindsay and her chauffeur were later executed by the IRA, and they burned down her home, Leemount House in Coachford.

In Dublin, the British Army on patrol took to bringing an IRA prisoner along with them in the back of their open-top patrol lorries to deter grenade attacks.

Mary Lindsay confronted by the IRA

BOMB US NOW!

British soldiers carrying an IRA prisoner to deter attacks

1921 The Empire Strikes Back

The British fought back with more and more internment and executions of IRA members. Informants helped the British bring back law and order. Three British soldiers were found dead on the Clare/Galway border with a sign from the IRA around one of their necks: 'Spies. Tried by court martial and found guilty. All others beware!' The Squad continued their assassinations against the RIC and informers in Dublin.

British spies killed by the IRA

British authorities carried out systematic curfews in

certain areas of Dublin and went door to door raiding each house. In Limerick that March, the curfews and raids resulted in British intelligence agent George Nathan shooting dead the Mayor of Limerick, George Clancy, former Mayor Michael O'Callaghan and IRA man Joseph O'Donoghue in their homes.

Fighting intensified throughout the country as the spring wore on. The first six months of 1921 would be the bloodiest of the war.

British soldiers carrying out door-to-door searches

1921 Dev Puts His Foot Down

De Valera's return to the Dáil saw him try to bring some order back into the chaos of the War of Independence and the IRA. In March, the Dáil officially declared war on the British administration (just in case it wasn't clear enough) and in April the IRA was reorganised to become closer to a regular national standing army. There had been tensions between Michael Collins and Cathal Brugha over the running of the IRA. Brugha was the Minister of Defence but the IRA looked more toward Collins for leadership.

In May, elections were held for Northern and Southern Ireland. Sinn Féin just used it as an election for Dáil Éireann and continued with the second Dáil once they were re-elected.

THE IRISH REPUBL
DECLARES WAR
ON BRITAIN!

I'M PRETTY SURE THEY GOT THE MESSAGE...

Dev declaring war on Britain

IT'S NOT MY FAULT THEY LOOK UP TO ME!

ISN'T IT?

Tensions ran high between Collins and Brugha over the running of the IRA

WE WILL BEHAVE LIKE A PROPER ARMY AND MARCH ON DUBLIN LIKE 1916!!

YEA AND DO YOU REMEMBER HOW THAT ENDED!!

Dev had a totally different approach from Collins

1921 Attack on the Custom House

D e Valera wanted to move away from the hit-and-run murderous tactics the IRA had been employing and proposed a proper public show of force against the British Army by capturing the Custom House in

The Custom House, Dublin

Dublin, a British administrative building. Michael Collins objected, knowing the British to be the superior fighting force in prolonged fighting of this style ... but he was overruled.

   The attack on the Custom House in late May was brief and disastrous. After the initial occupation, the IRA, led by Oscar Traynor, were outgunned very quickly so they set the building on fire. Eighty IRA men were captured, and the Custom House was gutted by fire, along with centuries of local government records (making my job all the more difficult). It was a huge blow to the IRA as they were quickly running low on supplies and soldiers.

Oscar Traynor

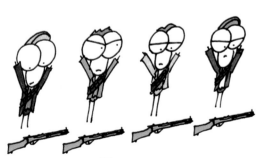

IRA men surrender after the disastrous Custom House attack

83

1921 Call for Peace

ULSTER IS OURS!

James Craig, Prime Minister of Northern Ireland

THIS IS A GREAT AND CRITICAL OCCASION IN THE HISTORY OF THE SIX COUNTIES — BUT NOT FOR THE SIX COUNTIES ALONE, FOR EVERYTHING WHICH INTERESTS THEM TOUCHES IRELAND, AND EVERYTHING WHICH TOUCHES IRELAND FINDS AN ECHO IN THE REMOTEST PARTS OF THE EMPIRE.

King George V's address to Northern Ireland

WE CAN ALL LIVE HAPPILY EVER AFTER WITHIN THE EMPIRE! SEPARATE PERHAPS... BUT HAPPY!

Jan Smuts, Prime Minister of South Africa

CAN'T WE ALL JUST GET ALONG?

Pope Benedict XV

As attacks and reprisals from both sides intensified further during May, Pope Benedict XV urged the English and Irish to come to an agreement. In June, the British government declared that house burnings were no longer acceptable reprisal methods – better late than never! James Craig, one of the main advocates of the Ulster Covenant back in 1912, became Prime Minister of Northern Ireland. King George V addressed the Northern parliament, calling for 'all Irishmen to pause, to stretch out the hand of forbearance and conciliation, to forgive and to forget, and to join in making for the land they love a new era of peace, contentment, and goodwill.' This speech was advised by South African Prime Minister Jan Smuts, a friend of the king. He believed Ireland could be a dominion of Britain like South Africa, Canada or Australia.

Stormont, the North's parliament building. Construction began in 1922

84

1921 Truce!

In June, the British government decided to call a truce with the Irish government. The attempt to establish a Home Rule parliament for Southern Ireland had failed miserably. More and more people were being killed, more and more money was being spent and, from what the British could see, the

IN VIEW OF THE CONVERSATIONS NOW BEING ENTERED INTO BY OUR GOVERNMENT WITH THE GOVERNMENT OF GREAT BRITAIN, AND IN PURSUANCE OF MUTUAL CONVERSATIONS, ACTIVE OPERATIONS BY OUR FORCES WILL BE SUSPENDED AS FROM NOON, MONDAY 11 JULY

The order issued to IRA members throughout the country

IRA and their tactics would not be defeated anytime soon (little did they know how worn out they were at this point). They were at a stalemate and the fighting had to stop. Increasingly, negative international attention was being drawn to the conflict, something Britain did not want.

Lloyd George wrote to de Valera and they agreed on a truce, which was signed in Dublin on 9 July to come into effect on 11 July. On 10 July, the IRA killed two policemen in Belfast, sparking huge sectarian riots, which led to 16

civilian deaths and the burning of over 160 houses, most of which were Catholic homes. This would be Belfast's Bloody Sunday.

The Truce came into effect nonetheless, despite sporadic violence around the country, which would eventually calm down, but not in the North!

Bloody Sunday in Belfast

85

1921 Negotiating the Anglo-Irish Treaty

The next task was for the Irish and English to negotiate a treaty. Throughout the summer Dev and Lloyd George argued over whether or not Britain was negotiating with a sovereign state, with Dev as its president. Dev didn't get his way and eventually sent a team of negotiators to London in October, led by Michael Collins and Arthur Griffith.

LADS, IT'S AN AWFUL LOT OF PAPERWORK!

A Republic or a 32-county unified Ireland was never on the cards. The negotiations led to the Anglo-Irish Treaty, which created the 26-county Irish Free State,

(L-r): Arthur Griffith, David Lloyd George, Michael Collins (sporting a moustache) and Winston Churchill.

which would become a dominion of the British Empire. The English king would still be head of state and the Irish government would have to pledge the oath

THE TREATY PORTS

UNITED KINGDOM OF GREAT BRITAIN AND NORTHERN IRELAND

IRISH FREE STATE

Map of Ireland, the UK and the Treaty Ports of Lough Swilly, Berehaven and Spike Island.

of allegiance to the Crown. Three Irish ports would also be held by the British Navy: Lough Swilly in Co. Donegal, and Berehaven and Spike Island in Co. Cork.

The Treaty also allowed Northern Ireland to opt out of joining the Free State, cementing partition on the island.

The treaty was signed in December and Collins and Griffith brought it back to Dublin to a mixed response, to say the very least ...

1921-1922 Debating the Treaty

NO IRISH FREE STATE!! WE WANT A REPUBLIC!!

BUT IT WILL BE A STEPPING STONE TO FULL INDEPENDENCE!!

Dev and Collins debating the Treaty

In the Dáil, the Treaty was debated and people were divided! The likes of de Valera and Cathal Brugha were against the Treaty, believing it to be a betrayal of the Republic and that an oath of allegiance to the Crown was not acceptable. Collins, along with others, argued that the Free State was a stepping stone towards complete independence, giving them 'the freedom to achieve freedom'. Also, a renewed war with Britain would be unpalatable.

Ultimately in January 1922, the Dáil voted in favour of the Treaty, 64 votes to 57. De Valera and his supporters left in protest. In Dev's absence, Arthur Griffith was elected as President of the Dáil. Because the Treaty had to be ratified by the British Parliament of Southern Ireland, the Pro-Treaty TDs took their place as MPs for once, thus forming the Provisional Government of the Irish Free State, with Michael Collins as Chairman. Dublin Castle and many other places of authority were surrendered to the Free State.

LONG MAY IT LAST.

The Irish tricolour flew above many buildings as the British relinquished control

COME ON, GENTLEMEN. WE'RE LEAVING!

DON'T DO THIS, DEV!

Anti-Treaty members left the Dáil in protest

1922 More Sectarian Violence in the North

Meanwhile up North, sectarian violence in Belfast continued and membership of the IRA's Belfast Brigade increased significantly. While the Treaty was being discussed, Tyrone and Fermanagh's county councils pledged their allegiance to Dáil Éireann. James Craig had those councils shut down by the RIC.

Michael Collins was still calling the shots with most of the IRA in the North, assuring them that partition would be only a temporary measure towards a united Ireland. Belfast IRA leader Joe McKelvey was not convinced and left to join the anti-Treaty IRA in Dublin.

THE NORTH WILL NOT BE LEFT BEHIND!

Joe McKelvey

Loyalist attacks on Catholics continued, especially in Belfast. More and more people were being killed. The IRA responded with more attacks on police. Things were escalating. Fr Bernard Laverty, who was chairman of the Belfast Catholic Protection Committee, sent a telegram to Winston Churchill, saying that Catholics were 'being gradually but certainly exterminated'.

CAN THEY NOT JUST KEEP CALM AND CARRY ON?

Churchill reading Fr Bernard Laverty's letter

TAIGS AREN'T WELCOME HERE!

Sectarian violence continued in the North

1922 An Army Divided, a Nation Divided

In the South, the IRA was deeply divided about the Treaty. The pro-Treaty IRA began to be reorganised into the Irish National Army. Tensions rose as anti-Treaty IRA began capturing RIC barracks around the country as they were abandoned by British troops. That March, in Limerick, things came close to blows between pro- and anti-Treaty IRA as they took control of New (now Sarsfield) Barracks. They compromised, dividing the garrisons between them, but it was not to last.

De Valera travelled around Munster, speaking out against the Treaty and rousing the people to fight. IRA leaders met and decided to reject the Treaty and the authority of the Dáil, forming their own Army Executive of 16 men led by Liam Mellows, Rory O'Connor and Joe McKelvey.

In April 1922, they led 200 anti-Treaty IRA men to occupy the Four Courts in Dublin, hoping to get a reaction from British forces that had yet to leave the city. They'd made their move and awaited the response of the Free Staters.

COME ON, LADS! WE HAVE FOUGHT SIDE BY SIDE! NOT FOR THIS!

Anti-Treaty and pro-Treaty forces at loggerheads in New Barracks, Limerick

Collins and the Irish National Army. Note - there were more than four ...

THEY WOULD HAVE TO WADE THROUGH IRISH BLOOD, THROUGH THE BLOOD OF THE SOLDIERS OF THE IRISH GOVERNMENT AND THROUGH, PERHAPS, THE BLOOD OF SOME OF THE MEMBERS OF THE GOVERNMENT IN ORDER TO GET IRISH FREEDOM!

Dev in Thurles

Liam Mellows, Joe McKelvey and Rory O'Connor at the Four Courts

89

1922 Civil War Looms

UP THE REPUBLIC!!

Anti-Treaty forces taking control of Kilkenny

In May, anti-Treaty Republicans took over Kilkenny, forcing troops to arrive from Dublin. After a firefight and close to 20 casualties, a truce was called. This truce was solidified by pro- and anti-Treaty leaders in the Dáil.

The election was coming up in June for the 26 counties. Because Sinn Féin this time would be up against other parties such as Labour, Collins and de Valera decided to hold Sinn Féin together and not split the vote. They made a pact that pro- and anti-Treaty Sinn Féin candidates would form a coalition government whatever the outcome.

THIS IS TOTALLY GONNA WORK...

An unholy alliance

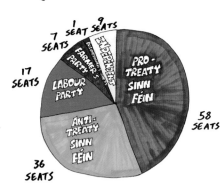

1 SEAT
9 SEATS
7 SEATS
FARMER'S PARTY
INDEPENDENTS
PRO-TREATY SINN FÉIN
17 SEATS
LABOUR PARTY
ANTI-TREATY SINN FÉIN
58 SEATS
36 SEATS

1922 general election results

Pro-Treaty Sinn Féin received 239,193 votes and anti-Treaty Sinn Féin received 133,864. Other parties received 247,226 votes and with the exception of the Unionist Party, the other parties were all pro-Treaty. The prospect of more war with Britain was not appealing, but it looked like war was coming either way!

1922 The Civil War Begins

Assassination of Sir Henry Wilson in London

Michael Collins was facing more and more pressure from Winston Churchill who was overseeing the transition period of Ireland. Sir Henry Wilson, a Longford man, former WWI commander and Northern Ireland security adviser, was assassinated by two IRA men in London in retaliation for the killing of Catholics in Belfast. Churchill believed these men were connected to the anti-Treaty IRA still occupying the Four Courts (although in reality they may have been sent by Collins himself). Churchill warned that if Collins did nothing about the rebels in the Four Courts, Churchill would send in British troops to retake it!

Collins gathered two British 18-pounder field guns and on 28 June 1922 brought the Free State Army to the Four Courts and opened fire, beginning the Battle of Dublin and the Irish Civil War. It was no longer the Irish fighting the British. It was former comrades, former brothers and sisters in arms, fighting against each other.

OPEN FIRE.

Pressure from Westminster

IF YOU DON'T DO IT, WE'LL DO IT FOR YOU!

1922 The Battle of Dublin

The shelling of the Four Courts

I'LL TELL MUM WHERE YOU ARE.

DON'T BOTHER, TRAITOR!

Republicans captured after the fall of the Four Courts

The attack on the Four Courts lasted two days. The Free State forces shelled it for the first day and stormed the building on the second day. The British offered to bomb it from the air but Collins politely declined the offer, to reduce casualties. The shelling resulted in the Four Courts catching fire. The Republicans had been storing ammunition in the Irish Public Record Office, part of the Four Courts. When the fire reached the store there was a huge explosion and centuries of Irish censuses, wills, parish registers and other documents were destroyed forever (making many historians and genealogists cry to this very day). The rebels in the Four Courts surrendered and some of the leaders were captured but fighting across the city continued.

Oscar Traynor had led the IRA to occupy Sackville Street, taking over buildings and hotels along the north-east corner. The National Army began to close in, moving artillery into position. It was like 1916 all over again. Most of Oscar Traynor's crowd were able to escape but Cathal Brugha and some men stayed behind in the Hamman Hotel while the fires intensified. Brugha eventually allowed his men to surrender but he later emerged by himself, revolver in hand, to face the Free Staters alone. He was shot and later died. A street close by would later be named after him.

Oscar Traynor looking from a window onto Sackville Street

This brought the Battle of Dublin to an end on 5 July. Many on both sides had been killed. Well over 250 civilians had been killed and 400 Republicans captured. The Free Staters were now in control of the capital.

GOD SAVE IRELAND...

Cathal Brugha's last stand

1922 The Fire Spreads

When fighting broke out in the capital, there was a mad scramble for control across the country between the Free Staters and the Republicans. When the IRA split, more had gone to the Republican side (12,000 v. 8,000 Free State). The Republicans also had the more experienced guerrilla fighters but lacked decent weaponry. The Free State Army, however, had direct access to the weaponry

Republican forces take over Ballymacool House, Letterkenny

LET'S BE CAREFUL ABOUT THIS, LADS!

of the British Empire and used it to their advantage.

Armagh man Frank Aiken, one of the commanders of the Northern IRA, said the Northern Division of the IRA would remain neutral, seeing the sectarian divides at first hand and how partition was very much a reality. Aiken would later be arrested with his men and taken to Dundalk prison.

Frank Aiken

Limerick man Liam Lynch had been captured in the Four Courts but was allowed to leave the city to convince his fellow Republicans to stand down. Lynch became chief of staff of the IRA and actually began organising Republicans around the country, heading first to Limerick. They strengthened their positions mainly in the south and south-west, nicknamed the 'Munster Republic'.

LADS, THEY LET ME GO!! NOW WE MUST GET READY TO DEFEND THE REPUBLIC!!

Liam Lynch makes his way back to Limerick

Free State armoured car

Assault on the Munster Republic

INCOMING!!!

Artillery gave the Free
State Army a huge
advantage

Because the IRA were under-equipped with weapons, Liam Lynch chose to take a defensive position in Limerick and let the Free State Army come to them.

Limerick

The National Army began recapturing towns throughout Leinster. Galway was captured with little resistance. Fighting broke out in Limerick between anti-Treaty and pro-Treaty forces and the National Army arrived, led by Eoin O'Duffy to reinforce the pro-Treaty forces. Fighting on the streets went on for over a week but Limerick was eventually captured by the Free State. Liam Lynch retreated to Clonmel. The same

WE WILL
HAVE ORDER!

Eoin
O'Duffy

day, Free State forces captured Waterford, the other corner of the Munster Republic.

Much like the British in 1916, the use of artillery gave the Free Staters a huge advantage against Republicans besieged in barracks. The Republicans had no choice but to abandon their positions to avoid capture. Not all the Free State forces were as experienced as those IRA, who had been fighting for years. They would discover this at Kilmallock.

The Munster Republic

95

1922 Battle of Kilmallock

After the fall of Limerick, Free State forces, led by O'Duffy, moved south towards Kilmallock, close to the Cork border, but Republicans were waiting for them.

On 23 July, the Free State captured the village of Bruff outside Kilmallock but the IRA were quick to take it back, taking 76 prisoners in the process. This first wave of Free State soldiers were inexperienced and were up against some of the most seasoned IRA fighters. Free State reinforcements arrived and Bruff was retaken but Republican forces hampered their movements with ambushes.

Over the next few days, another village, Bruree, was fought over by the two armies. The IRA attacked with three armoured cars and machine guns but were pushed back as even more Free State reinforcements arrived.

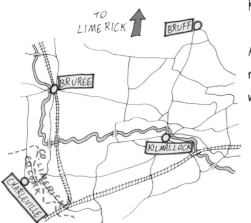

Kilmallock was there to be captured.

When the Free Staters arrived on 3 August, most of the Republicans had retreated to Charleville and beyond. They were needed elsewhere!

An improvised armoured car converted from a coal truck by the Republicans

SHE MAY NOT LOOK LIKE MUCH, BUT SHE'S GOT IT WHERE IT COUNT

The Tightening Grip of the Free State

Free State troops had travelled by sea and landed in Fenit, Co. Kerry, opening up a new front for the Munster Republic. A major difficulty for the Republicans was that they weren't fighting the British Army

Free State reinforcements arriving by sea

any more! The public had mainly supported fighting against foreign invaders, but fighting against an Irish army was not so popular. The Catholic Church, in particular, spoke out against the rebels and called for peace, and in the deeply Catholic society, this weighed heavily on many fighters. Ultimately, many chose not to fight or destroy roads, making things all the more difficult for defending against the Free State.

I HAVE TO LIVE IN THIS COUNTRY AFTER ALL THIS IS OVER! I'M NOT GONNA DESTROY IT!

Some Republicans abandoned the cause

Around the country, Republican activity was mostly confined to sporadic attacks against Free State soldiers.

The Free State Army continued recruiting more and more soldiers. Some veterans of the Great War joined up, bringing experience of a regular army, but mainly inexperienced men joined. By the end of 1922 the Free State Army would swell to 38,000 troops.

BETTER THAN THE TRENCHES AT LEAST!

Great War veterans joined the National Army too

1922 Republicans on the Back Foot

Harry Boland found in the Skerries Grand Hotel

Jailbreak in Dundalk

In Skerries, Co. Dublin, Harry Boland was shot while being arrested and died soon after. In Dundalk, Republicans blew a hole in the wall of Dundalk prison using dynamite, freeing many prisoners, including Frank Aiken. On that same day, Oscar Traynor was captured by Free State forces. Just over a week later, a Republican plot to blow up the bridges leading out of Dublin was foiled and a huge portion of the remaining Dublin IRA was captured. In Munster, Free State troops landed via boat in Youghal and Passage West, just outside Cork city. They met heavy gunfire as they approached the city but the Republicans ultimately abandoned Cork city, leaving it to the approaching Free State forces on 10 August.

As Free State forces closed in, Liam Lynch abandoned the town and ordered all other IRA forces to go back to guerrilla warfare. They couldn't fight the Irish National Army head-on any longer. It looked as if victory was near for the Free Staters!

WE CAN'T HOLD MUNSTER! IT'S BACK TO THE OLD TACTICS!

Liam Lynch calling for a change of tactic

1922 The Death of Arthur Griffith

he weight of setting up the Free State Government and the outbreak of Civil War took its toll on its President, Arthur Griffith. He died of a brain haemorrhage in Dublin on 12 August 1922. William T. Cosgrave, who had escaped the executions of 1916, became the new President of the Free State.

This stressful period took its toll on Arthur Griffith

The guerrilla attacks continued throughout August. Monaghan and Carrick-on-Shannon saw Republican attacks. Frank Aiken led an attack on the barracks in Dundalk, capturing the town. Around 240 prisoners were released and 400 rifles were captured, but they withdrew from the town once they got what they needed. Republican forces along the border with Northern Ireland began to use the border to their advantage, fleeing across it where the Free State army couldn't follow them.

I HATE TO SEE THE COUNTRY TEARING ITSELF APART!

Frank Aiken in Dundalk

THE NORTH

THE FREE STATE

Sneaking across the border

1922 The Death of Michael Collins

SURE THEY WON'T KILL ME IN MY OWN COUNTY!

As the Free State seemingly tightened its control of Munster, Commander-in-Chief Michael Collins decided to travel down to his home county of Cork, despite strong advice against it.

He went to Cork city and met neutral IRA members to try and make contact with anti-Treaty IRA, to sue for peace. On 22 August he travelled from Cork city to tour through west Cork, possibly to meet with de Valera, who was possibly in the vicinity at the time. While passing through Béal na Bláth, he was recognised by an IRA man. After Collins and his convoy drove on, an ambush was planned in case the convoy returned that day.

That evening the Free State convoy returned through Béal na Bláth where the IRA was waiting. A gunfight ensued and Collins was shot in the head, the only man to die in the ambush.

His body was later brought to Dublin by sea and lay in state in City Hall, mourned by tens of thousands of people. He was 31 years old and left behind his fiancée, Kitty Kiernan. His state funeral temporarily brought the warring factions together in mourning. But this was not to last.

Ambush at Béal na Bláth

1922 The War Turns Bitter

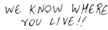

A rthur Griffith and Michael Collins were dead. Collins had been the closest link between the two sides, wanting to bring about peace and forgiveness and get on with running their own country. But with those two relatively moderate leaders gone, the Free State leadership grew bitter towards the Republicans, who would just not surrender! Things once again descended into attacks and reprisals, sometimes brother fighting brother. Both sides became more ruthless and merciless in their killings.

Both sides became more and more ruthless

W. T. Cosgrave and Richard Mulcahy

In September, the Public Safety Bill was passed by the Dáil, allowing the National Army to run military courts to imprison or execute men bearing arms against the state or aiding any attacks made against the state. Days later, at the start of October, the Free State offered an amnesty to IRA fighters who surrendered, but that did not work.

1922 Women in the Civil War

I BET YOU KNOW LOTS OF IMPORTANT SECRETS, DON'T YOU?

Cumann na mBan chose to fight against the Treaty and the Free State, believing the Republic to be the best vehicle for women's rights. They had already come far in the wars. There were women judges in the Dáil courts and the 1921 election had seen six women TDs.

TIME TO GO FIGHT FOR THE REPUBLIC!

During the Civil War, Cumann na mBan led their own attacks against Free State operations. They were particularly useful to the IRA for gathering information from Free State sources; they had their methods. Cumann na mBan ran crèches in Dublin, which allowed mothers to continue the fight during the day.

The Provisional Government of the Free State outlawed the organisation in October. The Catholic Church and media began speaking out against these upstart women, and society saw it as unseemly for a woman to break from traditional gender roles. There was (and still is) a long way to go for women's rights in Ireland.

TDs Constance Markievicz, Mary MacSwiney and Margaret Pearse

1922 The Executions Begin

In November the Free State began executing IRA prisoners. They executed head of Republican propaganda Robert Erskine Childers, who had previously helped negotiate the Treaty and smuggle guns aboard his yacht, 'Asgard', into Howth

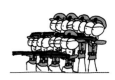

TAKE A STEP OR TWO FORWARD, LADS! IT WILL BE EASIER THAT WAY!

The execution of Robert Erskine Childers

back in 1914. The IRA declared they would assassinate every TD who voted for the Public Safety Bill and started with Sean Hales on 7 December. TD Pádraig Ó Máille was also wounded. In retaliation, the Free State executed

Rory O'Connor, Liam Mellows, Joe McKelvey and Richard Barrett, all of whom had been held since the taking of the Four Courts. Because their arrests were before the Public Safety Bill was brought in, their executions were technically illegal, but it was tit-for-tat!

The shooting of Sean Hales and Pádraig Ó Máille

Liam Mellows, Joe McKelvey, Rory O'Connor and Richard Barrett were executed by the Free State

1923 Violence and Atrocities

As 1923 began, the Republican guerrilla war continued. They burned the homes of TDs and others connected to the Free State. They also burned the old 'big houses' of Anglo-Irish families, the former Protestant ruling class. The chaos of the Civil War was a time when many old grudges were settled and atrocities against old enemies were committed. Prisoners of the IRA were taken to the middle of nowhere and shot, sometimes left to bleed to death.

That March, in Co. Kerry, five Free State soldiers were killed by a Republican booby trap at Knocknagoshel. The next day, the Free State army used Republican prisoners to search for landmines. That night, they tied nine prisoners to

A country ravaged by civil war

Ireland had plenty of quiet corners to carry out violent acts against the enemy

a landmine and detonated it. One man was blown clear to freedom; the other eight were blown apart or shot. The vindictive violence in Kerry and across the country would continue, much to terrible public outcry.

Republican prisoners strapped to a landmine

1923 The End of the Civil War

NO COMMUNION FOR YOU, COLM!

With the increasing executions of IRA members and ever-depleting weapons, the Republican fight was waning. The Catholic Church had stopped administering the sacraments to known IRA members, and the power of Catholic guilt is not to be underestimated!

I'VE LOST CONTROL OF THEM!

De Valera wanted a ceasefire but he had no control over the IRA, who had voted to continue the war. In April, the Free State killed Liam Lynch, the IRA chief of staff, and captured many of the IRA Executive in the Knockmealdown Mountains in Co. Waterford. Frank Aiken, who was captured, became the new chief of staff of the IRA. Aiken had always been a more practical and realistic leader and at the end of the month, he officially called a ceasefire. In May, he ordered all IRA members to dump their arms and stop fighting. Dev

Dev had lost his influence with the IRA

sent out a message to the troops: 'The Republic can no longer be defended successfully by your arms. Further sacrifice of life would now be in vain and the continuance of the struggle in arms unwise in the national interest and prejudicial to the future of our cause. Military victory must be allowed to rest for the moment with those who have destroyed the Republic.' The Free State had won.

SO THAT'S THAT, THEN!

1923 The Costs of War

Many Republicans were imprisoned

The Irish War of Independence saw more than 2,000 people killed: over 500 IRA, over 700 British forces and over 750 civilians.

The Civil War saw around 800 Free State forces killed and somewhere between 1,000 and 3,000 Republicans killed. The number of civilian deaths across the country is unknown, but around 250 civilians were killed in Dublin alone. The Free State made 77 official executions with possibly over 100 unofficial ones!

Because the war had ended, the 13,000 Republican prisoners who'd been arrested in wartime under emergency powers could now be released. Fearing fighting starting again, the Free State brought in more powers to hold onto these prisoners and began rounding up the others, even after they'd dumped their weapons.

William Cosgrave reorganised pro-Treaty Sinn Féin into a new party, Cumann na nGaedheal, and won the 1923 elections with 63 seats. Many Unionists in the south got behind CnaG, accepting they'd never have a majority in the south. De Valera was arrested while running for the election but he won his seat nonetheless, along with 43 other Republicans.

The Irish Free State

Denny Barry on hunger strike

The Free State was officially a reality. W. T. Cosgrave was the President of the Executive Council. The Civic Guard became the Garda Síochána, the new police force. In October 1923, with no sign of release, thousands of prisoners went on hunger strike. Denny Barry and Andrew Sullivan would die in November on hunger strike and the IRA called off the rest of the strike.

The Free State began to release the prisoners throughout 1924 with an amnesty to all Republicans granted by November that year. De Valera reorganised his Republicans into a new party, Fianna Fáil, to oppose Cumann na nGaedheal. They would later come to power in 1932 with a tense but thankfully peaceful and democratic transfer of power.

1930s Dev in the Aftermath

Over the next hundred years Irish politics would centre around Fianna Fáil and Fine Gael (formed from CnaG in 1933), two sides of the same coin that stemmed from the original Sinn Féin party. Power would go back and forth between the two parties, with people voting for who their father voted for. Both these parties being conservative resulted in Ireland being a deeply conservative country; that and the massive influence of the Catholic Church.

De Valera spent the 1930s dismantling the Free State from the inside (which is what Michael Collins had suggested before the Civil War!). Ultimately, he was able to end the Free State and create a new constitution, and established the newly independent Ireland (or Éire, in Irish) in 1937.

This constitution gave a special place for the Catholic Church in Ireland with huge influence from Archbishop John Charles McQuaid. The Church took on the running of the school systems and many other institutions. But those are stories for a completely different book!

WELL MY DAD VOTED FIANNA FÁIL AND SO WILL I!

OH YOU'RE ONE OF DEV'S LOT ARE YOU?

Civil War politics

The official symbol of Ireland

LET'S DEFINE THE ROLE OF WOMEN IN THE HOME!

AND THEN ONTO FAMILY MATTERS...

Writing the constitution of Ireland

Constitution of Ireland

YAY! WE'RE A REPUBLIC!!

1960s-1990s A Province Still Divided

Riots in 1969

In Northern Ireland, James Craig had established a 'Protestant state for a Protestant people'. Sectarian discrimination and violence in the North continued throughout the 20th century, escalating in the late 1960s to what became 'The Troubles', a war between Republicans, Unionists and the British Army. Much history repeated itself. There were more murders, more reprisals, another Bloody Sunday, more hunger strikes, the emergence of a new Sinn Féin republican party and this conflict would rage on until the mid 1990s.

IRA

Bloody Sunday, Derry, 1972

The Good Friday Agreement of 1998
established that if a majority in the North
and South wanted Northern Ireland to join
the Republic, the British government would
make it so. The British Referendum to leave
the European Union in 2016 resulted in the
UK voting to leave, although a small majority
of Northern Ireland voted to remain. This
began murmurs of a united Ireland
once again, with different parties
courting the idea throughout
2017 and beyond. Will the
border come down before it is
100 years old?

Unionist and Republican flags
flown in Northern Ireland

BUT WE
DIDN'T VOTE
FOR BREXIT!

BUT WE
VOTED
AS A WHOLE
COUNTRY,
NOT INDIVIDUALLY!
COME ON!
WE'RE GOING
TO BE
FREE!!

Statue of peace in Derry/Londonderry

Where Are We Now?

A hundred years on from the events of these Irish revolutionary times, it's interesting to see where Ireland is today. Civil War politics feels like it's on its way out. A more diverse, more informed electorate resulted in the 2016 general election being a much less clear-cut choice of party. Fine Gael won 50 seats, Fianna Fáil won 44, Sinn Féin 23, Labour 7, Anti-Austerity Alliance – People Before Profit 6, Independents 4 Change 4, Social Democrats 3, Green Party 2 and 19 for Independents. Even though the obvious choice was for Fine Gael and Fianna Fáil to form a coalition government together, Civil War politics dictated that they could not. So their best compromise was to have an unholy alliance where Fine Gael formed a minority government with some independents, wth Fianna Fáil in opposition but abstaining from votes of no confidence in the government, and keep new Sinn Féin from being the main party in opposition.

The joys of politics ... but at least they're not shooting each other!!

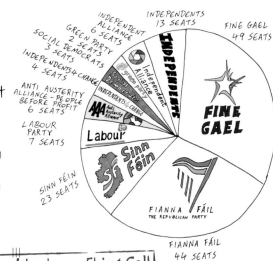

Fianna Fáil
and Fine Gael

First published in 2017 by

The Collins Press

West Link Park

Doughcloyne

Wilton

Cork

T12 N5EF

Ireland

A CIP record for this book is available from the British Library.

Hardback ISBN: 978-1-84889-333-7

Design and typesetting by Studio10
Typeset in Nothing You Could Say

Printed in Poland by Białostockie Zakłady Graficzne SA

Cover illustrations by John D. Ruddy

also available on YouTube

And many more! youtube.com/johndruddymannyman